THE LOVING

by

Robbie Moffat

PALM TREE PUBLISHING

PALM TREE PUBLISHING
Paisley, Scotland Pa1 1TJ

First published in paperback JANUARY 2019

Typeset: Verdana 10pt

ISBN-10: 0 907282 73 3
ISBN-13: 9780907282730

PREFACE

Love and romance, action and adventure, the ingredients of good story telling. What the writer fails to tell us, we have to fill in for ourselves.

And so it is with The Loving, a tale set in another age, in a gone-world of yesteryear, when there was war and plague everywhere, and relationships were cut-short by death, illness and madness.

DEDICATION

This book is dedicated to Pat Trevor.
Rest in peace.

Love's own air, mien, demeanour
betrays itself, comes to light ...
bearing, garb, complexion, colour
flushes forth, flares into passion
'til time dissolves, leaves no trace,
we lovers cease to be, fade out,
melt away, depart or flee ...
leave no shape or form behind.

1

In the year 1855 in Constantinople, the plague was prevailing, but not with any violence. Its presence, however, lent a mysterious and exciting interest to that great oriental city. It gave it tone and colour, a tone and colour sombre enough, but true, and well befitting the dreary monuments to past Ottoman power and splendour.

Turkey was sick. Its society had become associated with the plague. It dwelt with the faithful in the holiest quarters of the city. The ugly shaped and fashioned Pera coats and matching hats, they could be held to be innocent of infection, but the rich furs and costly shawls, the embroidered slippers and gold-laden saddle cloths - the fragrance of burning aloes and the rich aroma of patchouli - these were the signs that marked the familiar home of the plague.

*

Emil Osman was on leave from duties at Scutari to visit his parents. He had crossed the Bosphorous to Pera and now had to take another boat to reach the city, so he went down to the waterfront to take a caique across the Golden Horn. However, before his caique was quite ready to make the crossing, some rueful looking fellows came rapidly shambling down the steps with a plague ridden corpse which they were going to bury with the faithful on the other side of the water.

"Get him in" the boatman hissed "but he'll have to pay double."

The boatman howled at his own humour and slapped Emil on the shoulder.

"D'you hear that one, son" he cackled as if death were a laughing matter, and the plague a good source of business.

Emil found himself being touched by the men bearing the body as they got into the boat. Emil had not contrived to be in contact with the plague, but as the caique eased its way out into the dark waters of the Golden Horn, the foot of the dead man, lolling out of the bier, repeatedly brushed against his leg.

Emil had heard the debates as to whether the plague was passed on by contagion or not. He had finally come to the conclusion that it was, but had already taken on the view that what would be, would be. It had allowed him to lie amongst the dying in Scutari without the alarm and anxiety that otherwise would have pressed on his mind if he had allowed himself to believe that every passing touch was a probable death-stroke.

The caique came to rest in the mud of Stamboul. Emil leapt out the boat and left the funeral party to their task. He made his difficult way up a steep and narrow alley, shut in between blank walls, and little frequented by passers-by, and came upon a coffin-shaped bundle of white linen that passed for an Ottoman lady. Painfully struggling against the obstacles to her progression, interposed by the many folds of her clumsy drapery, by her big mud-boots, and her two pairs of slippers dangling from her arm, she worked her way on awkwardly ahead of him. Despite her ungainliness, there was something womanly in the labour and effort with which she tugged and lifted the burdens of her charms, closely followed by her women slaves. Of her very self he saw nothing, except the dark luminous eyes that stared against his face as he passed her, and the tips of her painted fingers dangling like the rosebuds in the Sultan's garden. She turned, and turned again, and carefully glanced around her on all sides to see that she was safe from the eyes of any other men, and then suddenly withdrawing the yashmak, she shone upon his heart and soul with all the pomp of her beauty.

Emil had learned to smile at pretty women - and to turn pale before a beauty that was great enough to have dominion over him.
Catching him thus, the woman with a sudden movement lay her blushing fingers on his uniformed arm and cried out "Yumourdjak! Here is a present of the plague for you!"
The lady's silvery laugh rang down the alley, and the cackles of her attendant women were boisterous. One in particular, who had discarded her veil, and who had the dark pleasing face of a Christian, laughed so loudly that Emil's attention was drawn to her. She had more life to her than

the volunteer nurses he had seen at the Military Hospital at Scutari, and certainly more appeal than any Turkish girl he had ever met. He had never seen such joy and happiness in the face of a woman. He studied her intensely; unaware of everything that had gone before. Her laugh enraptured him, and in an instant, their eyes met, but this was brought to an end by her mistress slapping her face and pulling her to the ground by her hair. She placed a large mud-boot foot on the girl's long tresses, pinning her to the ground.

"You Russian bitch! You are a whore. When we are home I shall teach you Turkish manners as you have never had from me before."
The mistress was shaking with rage, standing on her with her other foot, and stabbing her stomach with the full weight of her heavy leg. "This will pay you for Russians having warships on the Black Sea and the deaths at Sebastopol."

The Russian girl struggled free. She recovered her fallen black head cloth, and then began running along a side alley towards the main thoroughfare that headed in the direction of the Grand Bazaar. Emil, in a fit of impulse, followed her through the narrow alleys of the old city, keeping her just in sight. He was not aware that she knew he was following her until he lost her in a busy street inside the bazaar.
He looked everywhere.
The bazaar was crowded with people in

animated discussion selling or buying the merest trifles. One, a seller of olives, was demanding a price immensely beyond that which a customer was offering. It was no small consequence, said the seller, that he had waddled ashore with these olives which he had bought from a Greek brigantine now that he had reached this nook in the bazaar, he was putting his goods before the public, and himself upon them, and he would lay fire to his pipe and sit in permanence until he obtained the best price he could get on the open market.

Next to this man was an old pious Musselman, who sufficiently rich, seemed to be holding back his ware, maintaining a kind of judicial gravity, and receiving applicants to his stall as if they were suitors rather than customers. Emil could hear someone quietly end some long speech to him that concluded with an offer, only to be replied with a bold "Yok", which meant distinctly no.

Emil was catching a glimpse of the old Ottoman world. His life in the military was hardening his heart against the poetry of the past. For the conversations in the bazaar sounded like the language of the Arabian sands, embroidered with description, rich with oriental phrases, epitomising the Empire's absence of great capital and great credit, every seller in the bazaar importer, warehouseman, wholesale dealer, retailer, and shop man, each searching out a fair market value for his goods.

The Ottoman Empire was a waning power, a fading splendour that elicited laughter and mockery from the great powers of Europe. It was this lack of respect that initiated the despot of Russia, Csar Nicholas I, to declare his right of protection over all the Orthodox Christians in the Ottoman Empire. He had invaded the Empire and destroyed the Turkish fleet at Sinope, but the Turkish armies had driven his armies out again. Yet, the Allies, England and France, spoiling for a war, had used the conflict as an excuse to invade the Crimea and destroy the Russian fleet at Sebastopol.

Emil, along with a detachment from his battalion, had been posted to Scurari, to strengthen the Turkish Customs House that was housing the supplies to the Allies in Sebastopol. From the quay thousands of tons of food, equipment and ammunition was unloaded from ships from France and England. Most of it was reloaded on to the hospital ships that were bringing back the appalling casualties from the Crimea. The British and French had marched on to Sebastopol without cold-weather equipment and had dug in for the winter. Snow had blocked the roads and it had become impossible to forward supplies. Their horses had died of starvation, making the transport problem even worse. With inadequate nourishment and disgraceful sanitation, the Allied army suffered dreadfully from cholera as they daily tried to overrun Todleben's Russians who had managed to entrench one hundred and forty thousand men in a series of earthwork defences around the town. About half of the wounded that arrived at the Military Hospital at Scutari died of their wounds after a three-week journey back from the battlefront.

To Emil, it was a pointless war, nothing had been achieved, and a half a million men in the end had been killed or wounded. It would be another month before Spring finally arrived, when it was expected that an advance would be made by the Allies and Sebastopol taken. But in the meanwhile, even as a Turk, it was a sickening feeling to see the dead and the maimed being off-loaded from the hospital ships, for Scutari was rife with plague, and Emil was glad to be away from there for his seven days of leave.

Army life was not so bad, most times dull, and very rarely dangerous. Guard duty at the Customs House had not taxed him, the patrol work had been easy. It was not as if Emil was expecting to be called up to the battlefront. Marching on Russian soil in winter was his idea of suicide. Look at what had happened to Napoleon's army in eighteen-twelve. Six hundred thousand men to win the battle of Borodino, Moscow captured, then six hundred thousand in retreat from the Russian winter, only two thousand surviving. What did that signify?

To Emil it signified the folly of all wars, the subjugation of one nation over another. It proved that fighting achieved nothing but death and hardship and poverty, and that liberty was a thing that was granted, not taken away.

*

In the bazaar, Emil was brought back to the present with a jolt as a woman pushed him out of her way and carried on in a bustle through the crowd.

It was the girl!

Having first seen the servant girl, followed her, and then lost her in bazaar amongst the many head scarf-covered women, he had felt a sense of loss, a feeling of emptiness as he had scanned the crowds of people thronging in the covered streets of the market. Searching for her, hoping for a glimpse, watching for her, he prayed that he had not lost her for good amongst the inhabitants of the world's largest city.

Instead, she had been watching him. She had let him follow her all this time; now she led him on out of the bazaar, teasing him by taking endless unnecessary turns and twists down narrow alleyways and side-streets that seemed to lead in circles. At last, turning a tight corner, he came upon her sitting beneath an olive tree with her back to him.

There was no one else about. He hesitated momentarily, but the heat of the chase had hardened his desire to see her face again, and he approached her quietly, whistling the tune of a song he had learned in the army. He was aware of a warm breeze in his face, and as he moved closer to the olive tree, he perceived she had stopped at a spot that was well familiar to her, for she was totally at ease, and knew how to lean against the tree to maximise her comfort.

Emil had once had a tree like that in the garden of his parent's house before they had moved to a larger house in the city, but it had not been as old or as gnarled as the one the girl now lay against. He approached her from the side, but she did not look up
"Salem" he said to her in the softest voice he could coax from his choked throat.
"Salem, sir" she replied in a polite firm tone that seemed to stifle a laugh.
"What's your name?" he asked politely.
"You don't need to know that, sir, you've seen what I am." Her reply made Emil recall the incident with her mistress in the alley. "Come, no-one is looking, let me see your face again."
She turned away. He went up to her and drew back her yasmack, and all the beauty and radiance that Emil had first seen in her face in the alley, had been replaced by long pitiful tears of shame and humiliation. He was unsure what to do, but before he could stop himself, he had put an arm around her shoulder, and was wiping the tears from her eyes. She pushed him away.
"I am a human being" she half-cried "not some animal."
Emil had become used to seeing Christians treated worse than animals at the hospital in Scutari. Life was cheap, totally without value to the commanding officers of the British and French armies. He had never

seen such disregard for human life. Even the Chief medical Officer of the English had said he'd rather see his patients die than be treated by the English nurses trying to organize the laundry and sanitary conditions of the wounded.

"I have seen animals treated better than people" he said, consoling her. "Not all Muslim ladies are like your mistress." Emil was thinking of his own mother, a woman of forty-five who maintained three cats, a dog, and some love birds.

"There's also a war going on ..."

"But they don't have to take it out on me because I'm Russian. I hate the Csar as much as anybody."

Emil looked straight into her eyes as she spoke. He watched them fill with fire, with indignation for her country's plight, for all the wrongdoings of the Csar who was responsible for her own slavery and that of all Russian serfs.

Then, an overwhelming desire prompted Emil to do something he had never done before. As she went to open her mouth and say something further, he kissed her, kissed her on the lips, kissed her so passionately that she immediately responded in a way that took him totally by surprise. She did not struggle; she did not push him away, but attempted to suck his tongue into her mouth.

He drew back from her. Was she playing with him? He began to feel used.

"Please take me away from here" she pleaded.

"What?" stuttered Emil, feeling he was

going down a road he had no desire to walk.

"Help me to be free." She looked him with such a wanton, pleading expression, his resolve to remain detached melted a little, just a little. "I have no-one in the whole world to help me."

For the first time in his life Emil realised he was being asked to do a thing of honour. At the same time, he also realised that he might be about to say something he might regret and pay dearly for later. But how could he refuse? How could he walk away from this beautiful girl without saying another word? How could he reasonably explain that his life as a soldier was more important, that he loved his mother and father, that people were dying everywhere, and that it did not seem to matter whether a person lived in Stamboul or Moscow, life was all miserably the same if you were poor, no matter which country you were from. But he could not bring himself to tell her that - this Christian girl with long brown hair and brown eyes and dark skin who was so beautiful and did not know it.

Then before he had thought it through any further to say 'Yok', he said "Yes."

"Thank you!." she said coldly. She did not hug or kiss him like a female child who has received the thing she had been asking a parent or relative for half a day. She was too grown up for that.

"Now tell me your name?" demanded Emil. "Your name?"

The girl flickered her long eyelashes towards the tree above her, thought awhile, giggled, and said "Olive". It was not her real name. He real name was Vanya Kharkov, but because of her looks, her master had used Olive as a nickname for her to describe her dark moods and personality.

"Olive" Emil laughed "What sort of name is that?" he teased. But he liked it just the same, and from that moment, it was the only name he came to know her by.

2

Grigori, a man who passed himself of as a Romany, was a man of massive stature who been born somewhere west of Sebastopol. He had deserted Taurida province in the wake of the war in the Peninsular and made for Odessa with the thousands of refugees happy to escape serfdom, travelling as he did, onwards into the Balkans, with a dancing brown bear he had won in a game of chance.

He had learned that Csar Nicholas was dead and that the new Csar, his son Alexander II, had pledged to reform Russia and emancipate the serfs, but Russians had heard that all before during the early reign of his father.

To Grigori, the government of Russia would always be an intellectual and social tyranny. The annual expenditure on the army was forty percent of the national budget. Because of serfdom there had on average been twenty peasant revolts a year during Nicholas's reign. Things had become so intolerable in Russia, serfs had even begun to commit offences in the deliberate hope of being sent to Siberia, though that involved a terrible march on which many perished or died in the unspeakable conditions of the Siberian mines. No-one knew for certain, but it was said that more than one hundred and fifty thousand had been ordered to Siberia as exiles by Nicholas. Certainly, no one could argue with the new Csar's belief that there was room for improvement of all kinds in Russia. Yet, the root trouble was the institution of serfdom, by which each peasant was bound to the soil. If unhappy with a serf, a lord could confine them in chains, flog them to death, or sell them into foreign slavery.

Grigori preferred not dwell on the past or give reasons to others why he had fled from Russia, for it had not been an easy journey. Yet, the war and the refugees had made it simpler to hide amongst the many. With so much unrest everywhere, no-one had challenged his right to freedom, and few if any, had stopped him to ask him where he was going.

*

Grigori had the bear on a rope and wherever he went he would gather enormous crowds. He had a small goatskin drum tucked under his left arm that he would beat with a stick held in his right hand. The bear rope was attached to a leather strap around his right wrist and as he beat the drum the bear would rear on it's hind legs and dance in circles. As the crowd roared in laughter, he would entertain them:

"This is Ivan, Csar of the Bears" he would call out. Grigori had made a uniform for Ivan and a little hat that imitated the crown of a csar. "His father danced before Napoleon when he captured Moscow. The sight of a Russian bear was too much for Napoleon and it sent him scurrying home again without his army." The crowd roared with laughter "Like his father, Ivan has danced before princes and counts. Look into his big black eyes and see the splendour of the Russian court, the gilded furnishings, the sumptuous tapestries, the beautiful woman awaiting the return of their gallant cavalry officers from the wars with the English and French. Like you, madam."

An ugly peasant woman of indeterminable age, transfixed by the dancing bear, suddenly found her cheek kissed by Grigori. The crowd roared with pleasure. "But don't come too close, for Ivan is a wild creature that would sooner wrestle with a man than shake his hand. With one stroke of his powerful fore-paw, he can smash a man's skull." Some of the spectators moaned in awe at this thought. " Yet, he will let a child stroke his fine noble head and nestle into the bosom of a mother as if he were a child himself. I tell you, my friends, he is like myself - meek and tender when loved, but wild and uncontrollable when scorned and derided. So, spare some of your change for a travelling man and his companion, bring your children to stroke the head of Ivan for good luck, and they will live to tell their grandchildren about Ivan the Dancing Bear."

Grigori had owned Ivan for about a year. He was tired of caring and tending the animal. With a bear he could not live a normal life. Most times he had to sleep outdoors with him. Sometimes Ivan would get into bad moods and refuse to do anything. On one occasion he had fought with Ivan and they had nearly killed each other. Another time, when working on a Bulgar farm during the harvest, Ivan had become jealous of Grigori when he had taken a woman into a haystack. Left tied up, Ivan had broken free, sniffed about for his master, found the woman on top of Grigori, and slashed her across her bare rump with his claw. Grigori had been so angry, he had borrowed a pistol and led Ivan into the woods. He had put the pistol to Ivan's head, but the bear, staring back at him with it's big black eyes, had grunted and tried to lick the gun. Grigori could not pull the trigger, and rather than have someone else do it, he had left the harvest work behind, and moved on, taking the bear with him.

Thus Grigori had made his way through the Balkans to Belgrade like some low budget excursionist, seeing sights he had never seen before. In Russia the building of railways had only just begun, but in Belgrade there were four tracks leading out of the city.

As a Russian he was welcomed by the Serbs because of Russia's traditional hatred of the Turks, for Serbia was still garrisoned by the Turks, and no where more heavily than in Belgrade, dominated by the mighty castle on the banks of the river Save.

To avoid trouble with the Turkish forces that policed the city, Grigori passed himself off as a Romanian from Galatz, for there were many Russians settled in Romania content to live under Ottoman rule.

3

Emil had not told Olive that by eloping with her he was deserting the army. The Ottoman Empire was a big place anyway, and a man would have to very unlucky to be caught. Their plan was to travel on to Austria to seek asylum as refugees. Together they could start a new life together.

After some weeks, they had travelled as far as Nish, a major crossroads town in southern Serbia. They had run short of money and were arguing over how best to spend it. They had been blessed with a warm spring and an early summer, and lately they had been living off the land, labouring, travelling with other itinerants, sleeping out at night under the stars.

Now, in Nish, they found themselves in a large town unable to forage any food from the fields or gardens. To please Olive, Emil counted out the dinars they had left, made the decision that they should have a meal together in an inn. On other occasions, Olive had been opposed to such waste of their small savings, but tired of the rancour, and no longer strong enough to argue, she gave into his idea.

The inn they chose was The Damascus Soldier, a squalled wooden structure with mud-daubed walls and a roof of thatch. The interior was dark and smoky, no different from the inside of a dozen other such eating-houses, except for a large scimitar that was suspended from the roof by means of a rope tied firmly round its hilt.

"Yes, my friends" came a voice with an Egyptian accent from the gloom.

Emil peered to the back of the inn and made out a rotund man sitting at a table playing tavla with a smaller unkempt man.

"Food" said Emil in pigeon Turkish, not knowing what language he should speak in such unfamiliar surroundings.

"In a minute, friend" the large man replied as he rattled the dice in wooden cup and threw them on to the board.

Emil and Olive placed themselves on a wooden bench table and waited. They began to notice the other customers in the inn, all men, playing tavla, smoking their tchibouques, drinking coffee. All had turned to stare at them, first at Olive, but latterly at Emil, and they found their staring uncomfortable and menacing.

"She'll have to get over there with them." The small, unkempt Serbian man who had been playing backgammon with the Egyptian owner, had come to their table. Most of his teeth were gone and those that remained were black and broken, Olive looked over to the corner where he was pointing. Through the smoke she could see a small dark opening beneath a counter, out of which she could just see a pair of eyes staring her at.

"That's where the women go" said the table server. He took Olive by the sleeve and tugged her jalaba. Without protest she gave to the man's force and quickly found herself beneath the counter squashed against four other Muslim women. To save face, Emil laughed.

"Now, friend, what would you like" the shabby dressed little man asked him. "Rice with chicken, or without?" Emil ordered the chicken.

The waiter shouted out an order of "One chicken! One rice!" to some unknown cook at the back of the inn and took a jug of water off another table for Emil to wash his hand with. As he poured the water over his right hand, his food arrived on the table with a thud.

At that moment, another customer shouted "Mahmoud!" and the waiter scurried away to engage him in conversation.

Olive saw Emil look in her direction and give her a smile. That was all, there was no dark look of annoyance or irritation, he seemed content to sit there and be served. She had been thrown a bowl of plain rice and vegetables as if she were a dog. For the first time, she felt hatred for Emil. He had not protested at her treatment, he had laughed!

She had come to think of him as different from other Turkish men, but he was not, he accepted the customs of his country as if it were normal for men to treat women as animals. She recalled her first words to him - 'I am a human being, a Christian, not an animal'. She had thought that he had understood what she meant, but he had not. To be treated by a woman like an animal, as a slave, that is what he had understood her to mean. He had failed to grasp that most Muslim women where treated by men as slaves, the way her mistress had treated her. She had never told Emil the indignities her mistress's husband had subjected her too from the moment of her arrival in their house as a young girl.

He was a beast. It had been him who had taught her to suck in a man's tongue as if it were another part of his body. She had endured such violations to her own body from that same man without count, but she had never given her mind, never given up her dream of being free, and equal, if not greater, than any man could ever be.

When it came time to settle the bill, Mahmoud, in spite of the manner in which he had served the meal, asked Emil for a tip.

Olive was outraged at the man's temerity and her companion's timidity. Emil came over to her and asked her for the last of the change she possessed.

"You Turks never complain enough! Don't you how much it costs to put a dinner on the table!" hissed Olive pulling her yasmack up and leaning out from beneath the counter.

Emil tried to calm her. She did not

understand profit and overheads and wage bills the way he did, that's what he told her. Olive would not have any of it. She threatened to leave without him if he did not complain about the treatment she had received from the table server. Then, she pulled her black mask back down over her face, and once more, this time voluntarily, huddled away into the corner with the other women.

"I want to complain" Emil said boldly to the waiter Mahmoud.

The inn owner was called, a big round man of fifty, a veteran of Ibrahim Pasha's army that had conquered the whole area between Egypt and Turkey. He had a scar down his right cheek where he had been bayoneted at the battle for Damascus, hence the name of the inn.

"Yes, effendi, how can I serve you?"

The inn-keeper's face was not a pretty face to look into, but he was a man of considerable local standing in the town of Nish. He was viewed by some as a bully, yet to those close to him, he was a soldier hero. Ibrahim Pasha himself had decorated him.

Emil was scared. There was nothing wrong with the food; he just wanted to make a show in front of Olive in order to save face. He caught her watching him from the corner.

"Your man insulted my wife." He stressed the word wife as if it were the only word that would carry any importance. "He man handled her, and then had the nerve to ask for a tip."

The owner looked at his man Mahmoud who shrugged his shoulders.

"I saw nothing" said the owner "and it is customary in this inn to tip the waiter."

Emil could see he was going to have no joy from the Damascus soldier, but he could not lose face with Olive by paying a tip.

"I'm not paying any tip! The food was disgusting. I had better slops in the army!" Diplomacy seemed to be beyond him.

The inn-keeper shook his head as if he could not believe what he had just heard. His eyes rolled across his head and seemed to rest on Olive huddled in the corner with the other women. He grunted, and with a swiftness of movement that would not be possible for a normal man of his age, he grabbed Emil by the throat and squeezed the air from him.

"And which army would that be?" he hissed into the Turk's face. "Mahmoud, fetch the militia!"

Emil was aware of the shabby little table-server hastening out of the inn as he struggled to loosen the grasp of the innkeeper. Emil kicked over the table but soon found himself pinned on the floor by the innkeeper who had straddled him and commenced to knock his skull again and again against the earthen floor. Emil could feel blood in his mouth but he kept on struggling to overthrow the enormous beast of a man on top of him.

"Olive! Olive! Help me!" he whimpered.

The other women looked at Olive through the slits of their veils. She could see their dark sunken eyes, the depths to which they had accepted suffering, degradation and the contempt from their owners. They were little better than dogs huddled beneath a counter at the back of the inn. It was there that their bowls of food were thrown into them as they waited on their hands and knees to eat. Some were given nothing, left in the hole beneath the counter while their husbands or masters drank tea, smoked pipes, played backgammon for hours on end without concern.

During Olive's years of being among these Ottoman women, she knew they suffered indignities and humiliations that few other woman in the world had to endure. She did not know how she had learned this, but she knew it was so. She also knew that to step outside the bounds of her woman's world was punishable by stoning. To lift a hand against a man in the defence of another man was a crime. Emil was in trouble but she could not help him. She was not his wife. If she were his object, his property, than she would be want to do as he commanded, but she was neither of these. She was a Russian, and a Christian, who had been sold into slavery by her father's master. With Emil's help she had escaped from slavery, only to find that she was still being treated like a slave in the company of the man who had rescued her.

All this passed through Olive's mind in an instant. Perhaps she did love Emil, but love was a secondary thing to personal freedom and survival. As he shouted her name, she shrunk deeper and deeper into the recess of the counter, clinging to one of the other woman, not out of fear, but more out of a sense off detachment and non-involvement in the quarrel of people who were all foreigners to her.

Mahmoud returned with three men from the local militia. They were dressed as shabbily as the little waiter, but there was no mistaking their official duties as policemen.

"He's a deserter!" the Damascus soldier declared boldly "and I'll have my reward for capturing him."

4

Half an hour before the public execution outside the fortress in Belgrade, a large crowd had gathered to watch the spectacle, and found themselves being entertained by Grigori and his bear. Grigori had made a new costume for Ivan who was now dressed like the Sultan of Turkey. The crowd gathered round and laughed themselves silly at the sight of Ivan, appreciative of Grigori's political satire. Grigori knew he was taking a risk, but he had learned something about show business in his travels, and knew that Ivan's costume would draw the crowds.

This would be his last show, for if he was to travel on to Hungary and then Vienna, he could not take Ivan with him, for he had heard that street playing and begging was strictly forbidden in the Austro-Hungarian Empire and punishable by imprisonment. Therefore, until he managed to set himself up doing something in Vienna, he would have to live off what he made that day, and what he could get by selling Ivan.

Fifteen minutes into Grigori's and Ivan's act, two soldiers in red fez hats, one medium built and thin, the other medium built, fat, and sweating profusely in the sweltering heat, broke through the crowd and ordered Grigori to stop beating his goat-skin drum.

Grigori did not want to stop. In all his travels, he had never made so much money in so quick a time. The people of Belgrade were more than generous, throwing coins into his open travelling box, a surprise despite the tough authoritarian rule of the Turkish garrison stationed in the city's impregnable fortress. Without counting it, he could tell it was the best money he had ever made anywhere. He was near the climax of the show where he put his neck in the bear's mouth, and that of all their tricks, enticed people to dig deep into their pockets in appreciation. Thus, Grigori pretended he could not understand what the imperial soldiers were saying to him, and continued to perform his act and play his drum.

The soldiers were not amused by Grigori's indifference to them. Angered, the thin soldier un-shouldered his rifle, pulled back the bolt, and shouted to the crowd to stand back. The crowd directly behind the bear parted quickly. Grigori, sensing the danger, hastily stopped beating the drum, and reined in his bear. The soldier instructed Grigori to stand clear of Ivan. Grigori refused. The bear, still up on his hind legs, the tassels on his Sultan's costume bobbing to and fro, clung to Grigori's side The stouter soldier, red-faced and agitated, snatched at the bear rope round Grigori's wrist and pulled. The bear snarled and bared his yellow teeth. Grigori tried quieting the animal, but to no avail. Grigori knew that things had got out of hand. He had insulted the soldiers' ruler. He undid the rope round his wrist and let the line fall free. The bear dropped on all fours. The thin soldier took aim, and shot Ivan through the brain. The bear dropped dead and fell with a soft thud onto the baked earth.

A few of the crowd hissed, and then went silent. They crowded round Grigori to protect him.

The soldiers sized up the mood of the mob. There was genuine fear in their eyes. Prudently, they backed off, and retreated some distance away.

Grigori made a show of being angry. Some of the male spectators put their hands on his shoulders just in case he was thinking of trying to claw his way through the crowd in pursuit of the two soldiers.

"Don't be crazy, Russo" one hissed in his ear "they'll kill you like the bear. Look, there's their officer up there on the battlement - Major Ali - he is the one that orders all shootings. Do not move and he will not be able to single you out amongst us. They have their own internal problems today. After the executions you will be able to melt away in the crowd. "

A small group of curious citizens had gathered round the bear and were depositing coins in the travel case. They flung their coins in with expressions of "Death to the Sultan", "Turks Out of Serbia!" and other such phrases that underscored the hatred the people of Belgrade had for their overlords.

Grigori suddenly became aware of someone sobbing like a child. A waif like creature in Turkish dress was on her knees bent over his dead bear. Her black kashmak had been thrown back and he saw that she had a full head of thick brown hair. He was immediately attracted to her as her hair reminded him of that of some Ukrainian girls he had seen washing themselves in the Dniester river near Odessa.

"Forget your bear" someone said in his ear "take that girl to dance for you instead. She's here to see her Turkish lover-boy get it."

"Oh you poor creature" the girl muttered in Ukrainian, over and over again. Her speech was like that of a child and had the soft dialect of the Black Sea, but Grigori sensed she was talking to herself rather than to his dead animal. He knelt down and lifted her face from the black fur of the bear he had fed and companioned for eighteen months.

She looked straight into Grigori's eyes. Inside his heart raced. He had never seen such a pair of beautiful eyes in all his life. Perhaps he had been staring into Ivan's eyes for too long and had forgotten what the eyes of a woman really looked like, but no, the eyes of this girl were perfectly

formed, like two dark olives, ripe and pith
less.

"What's your name?" he asked her in
Russian.

"Vanya Kharkov" she stuttered in faltering
Ukrainian, surprised to hear from his lips
her native language spoken to her for the
first time in eight years. "But people call me
... Olive."

"Well, Olive Vanya Kharkov" he repeated,
so that he might not forget her name "Can
you dance?"

A crease crossed her forehead in an instant,
and Grigori suddenly imagined that he had
said something foolish and that the
information whispered in his ear had been
incorrect.

"A little ... but not like the bear." There was
a dark expression on her face and Grigori
thought he saw her trying to imagine what
sort of life it must have been for the bear
on the end of a rope. There was also an
ironic sense of humour. "Ivan's had a better
life than you or me" he said as he put his
hands under her arms and lifted her up.
She was incredible light, she was not too
tall, she had all the attributes of a born
dancer.

"Well, Miss Kharkov, my name is Grigori
Rostov, ex-director of the Sebastopol
ballet."

*

Emil had been taken from one guardhouse
to another with dozens of other men and it
seemed to him that they might have
forgotten him or mixed him up with some

of the others. But this had not happened. By the time they took him to Belgrade Fortress, they knew exactly who he was, his rank, his battalion, the length of time he had been in service. Although he had refused to give them his name, they called him Private Osman when they addressed him, and noted down every word that passed between them.

"Private Osman, you failed to return from leave to your battalion headquarters on the twenty third of March of this year. Is that correct." Major Ali, the presiding officer, at his court-martial asked him in a matter of fact way as if he had been asking these sort of questions all of his life.

Emil stood motionless and silent. Ali was not only a major in the Ottoman army, he was notorious for his ruthless persecution of Bosnian and Kosovan Christians. The Major, sitting bent over a table at the far end of the room which was in fact a prison cell large enough to contain forty men, did not look up. He sat like a stern schoolmaster, spectacles on the bridge of his nose, willing to be patient for a time and wait for an answer. Emil knew he was doomed no matter what he said and chose to remain silent. Without raising his eyes, the Major asked in a quiet voice: "Why did you run away?"

Emil was unable to say anything. To tell this man, notorious in Belgrade for his cruelty, that he had deserted the army for a servant girl would be humiliating. He did not want to hear his cruel laugh echoing in his ears when he went to the firing squad. But before Emil had time to finish his thoughts, Ali raised his head, pushed his spectacles on to his forehead, screwed up his eyes and looked intently at him.

"I know you, Osman" he said in an icy, measure tone, obviously calculated to scare Emil.

The sweat ran down Emil's back "You cannot possibly know me, Major, I have never seen you before" A pain ran all the way up his spine and numbed his brain.

"You are a Russian spy" he shouted out triumphantly to another officer in the room whom Emil had not noticed. He saw the flicker of cruelty in Ali's face as involuntary he began to stammer:

"No, Major, it is not true, you cannot possibly know me."

"You are a Christian working to overthrow Ottoman authority in Muslim Europe" Ali interrupted him.

"No" Emil lied "I am a Muslim student who has hardly ever been out of Constantinople!" Emil knew he had already been sentenced to death, but he did not want to be sent to the Major's torture chamber to end his life screaming. "Your name" Ali asked him with a change of tone that caught unguarded.

"Tabriz"

"What proof have I that you are not lying?"

"Sir!" exclaimed Emil in a tone of entreaty.

Ali lifted his eyes and gazed searchingly at him. For an instant they looked at one another, and the look saved Emil from the torture chamber. It was a look that went beyond the circumstances of a colonial officer acting as judge in the courtroom of an occupied country. It established human relations between them. Both of them were instantly aware of a number of things that united them against the world rather than against each other. They were both children of humanity and Turks. They were brothers but Emil was a deserter, and nothing could save him from the punishment metered out to deserters.

When Major Ali had first raised his head from the charge sheet where men's lives were numbers and Emil had been only a case, Ali could have had him shot without it weighing on conscience; but now he saw in Emil a human being. He reflected for a moment.

"How can you prove to me that you are telling the truth.?" said Ali coldly

Emil thought of Olive. She was the only one who could help him, but if he gave her as his witness - she was Russian and a Christian, then perhaps Ali would condemn them both as spies. He shrugged his shoulders. "You are not who you say you are, Private Osman."

The interview was over. Emil was led out, but where they were taking him he did not know. Ali was back at his desk looking at papers, and as Emil glanced back, he saw Ali sign a piece of paper and place it on a stack on his desk.

*

As Grigori put Vanya down, Grigori's hand brushed against one of her breasts. She did not seem embarrassed or coy. "You are an interesting one " he said to himself.

He guessed her age to be about eighteen. In fact, she was a sixteen-year-old adolescent from Kishinev whose serf guardians had sold her to a Turk called Tapiq from Constantinople when she was eight.

Olive guessed Grigori was twenty-two or three and divorced. In fact he was thirty and had never been married. From the look in his eye, she knew he liked her. In truth she had liked him from the moment she had set eyes on him. The man she had eloped with was about to be shot and she had to think about the future. Her soldier lover was a boy, but here was a real man, a Russian man who was everything that her Turkish boy was not. She had never danced in her life, but she would learn overnight if it meant this man would protect her and feed her.

The attention of the crowd had been diverted elsewhere. A column of Ottoman soldiers on either side of a row of five prisoners, all of them young men, marched out of the fortress gate. There were whispers amongst the crowd, and Olive, aware of the change of atmosphere, covered her head. Grigori held her close to him as he watched the column of soldiers line the condemned men up against the fortress wall.

Olive could feel his strength as he took her by the arm to steady her as the crowd surged forward. She could not see what was happening and felt trapped and claustrophobic in the midday heat.

Grigori could see everything clearly. Five soldiers had been tried by a military court, found guilty, and were to be shot. They were from all over the Ottoman Empire - a Syrian who had murdered a Serbian girl; a Macedonian who had stolen a rifle and sold it to a civilian; a Libyan who had stabbed a superior officer; an Albanian who had smuggled wine; and lastly, a Turk who had deserted his battalion in Constantinople.

Grigori's eyes fixed on the Turk. He was fair-haired and blue-eyed and no older than nineteen. He seemed to be searching the crowd for someone but he could not find them. What made a man desert? A young man like that should not have had a worry in the world. Back home his mother would cry her heart out for her disgraced son. Why had he done it? God knows.

A man placed his hand on Grigori's shoulder. It was the same man who had pointed out the Turkish officer to him. Grigori turned to see him motioning Grigori's attention to a cart harnessed to a well-fed looking mare standing a little way off. Along the side of the cart was a painted sign - Karadan Milosovic, Butcher.

The Belgrade butcher offered to buy the dead bear. Grigori asked to be paid in Austrian florins, but Milosovic shook his head and said that everyone was wanting florins or roubles or francs and that the best he could do was Turkish dinars. However, Grigori insisted that he had no use for dinars as he was hoping to cross the river Danube that night and go on into Hungary.

Milosovic smiled. "And her too" he asked with a dirty smile.

Grigori felt the girl's fingers dig into his arm. She would not have done that if she had wanted to be left behind. "Yes, her too."

"She'll need to get rid of that Muslim coffin-suit. If the Hungarians see her like that they'll know you've sneaked across the river in the middle of the night." He paused for a moment as the sound of a snare-drum role cut through his words. " I tell you what" he continued over the beating of the drum "maybe I can help you. Help me load the bear on to the cart, and then after the sport, we can go to my house and talk this business over further."

Grigori and the butcher loaded the unfortunate Ivan in his red sultan's suit on to the cart while Olive Vanya made furtive glances over the heads of the crowd. She could see nothing of Emil. The drumming stopped. "Are you coming up to watch then, girl?" Milosovic snapped at her. He was already on top of the cart steadying the horse with the reins.

Grigori was standing up at the rear of the cart. He reached down and offered her a hand.

"Get up you silly cow or you'll miss the fun" Milosovic yelled at her. "The stupid Turkish bastards are going to waste bullets and shoot all five at once."

*

The sun was in Emil Osman's eyes and the heat of the summer was intense. He could feel the heat radiating off the wall of the fortress behind him, the wall that in a few minutes would be splattered with his blood. He could hear the buzz of the flies milling about the Albanian who had a wound in his leg. He had been shot during his capture, but little had been done to cleanse his wound. A piece of army shirt had been used as a turnkey to stem the bleeding.

Of the others about to be shot he knew very little beyond their nationalities. He had passed the Libyan in the passage of the prison after his trial and exchanged quick glances. He had seen the look of fear in his eyes, and guessed from the Libyan's face, that he had seen the same thing in his. Now, as they stood in the heat of the Belgrade summer, he could hear the Libyan reciting from memory passages from the Koran.

The only other sound he was aware of was the voice of his mother in his head when he was a child in Stamboul - a sweet voice that consoled him through childhood illnesses, a stern voice that warned him of the evils in life. Where had he gone wrong? He felt like a stalk of corn caught in the wheels of a machine whose mechanism he did not understand but which worked without a hitch. He opened his eyes as he heard the scrape of the ramrods in the rifle barrels. Vainly he searched the crowd for the girl who had put him before the firing squad, but she was not there. Behind him on the battlements, the Major wiped his glasses. With a nod, the order to fire was given. The rifles went off, and he felt the heat of the ground and the sound of the flies as he fell.

5

Milosovic the butcher has a man in forties, stocky built, broad featured. He was a Serb who endured Turkish rule like a donkey endures a beating. He hated the Muslims. He was a Karageorgist nationalist who believed in a free Serbia, a greater Serbia that included Bosnia, Herzegovnia, Kosova, part of Bulgaria, and Macedonia. He was a supporter of K ara George's son, Alexander, who along with his nationalist associates, he was trying to bring to power. They were working to make the ruler of Serbia, Milosh Obrenovic, who's father had murdered Kara George, abdicate in favour of Alexander Karageorgovic. Or so Milosovic the butcher said.

To Grigori it was not very clear what was going on in Serbian politics, but his eyes told him that Belgrade was garrisoned by Turkish troops under the command of a Pasha. Whether the fellow whose butcher house he was now in with the girl had momentarily forgotten this, he could not be certain, but to get there they had passed through the lonely and desolate Moslem quarter of the city. They had gone up and down, and on, over shelving and hillocky paths barely wide enough for the cart; through lanes walled in by blank, windowless dwellings, until they had come upon an open space strewn with black ruins that some late disturbance had left; past a mountain of castaway things, the rubbish of centuries, and on until they had seen packs of wolf-like dogs lying torpid under the sun, limbs stretched out to the full, as if they were dead. As they crossed that open place and carried on upon the rutted track that led to a row of dwellings, cranes sat fearless upon the low roofs looking gravely down upon them, the still air they were breathing heavy with the scent of citron and pomegranate rind scorched by the sun, the smell of the approaching bazaar, dry, and dead from the perfume of stale spices.

Grigori had longed for some signs of life, the break of the ground now more heavy, the cartwheels turning noiselessly upon the crumbling soil of the city, the silence following behind them. Then they began to see turbans and the faces of men that had nothing for them - no welcome, no wonder as to where they were from, no wrath, no scorn; they looked upon them as if they were a December's fall of snow, seasonable, unaccountable, the uncomfortable work of God that may, or may not, have been sent for some good purpose, to be revealed to them later.

No -one came to greet them as they wound their way up to the butcher's home, a large rambling two story house in much need of repair, but by far a much more luxurious abode than any other in the near vicinity.

The butcher's wife received them with the smooth, gentle manner that belonged to well-bred Christians. She clapped her hands, and instantly the sound filled the lower end of the room with young children, her servants. A syllable dropped from her lips that conjured away the attendants like ghosts, their coming and going became swift and quiet as their feet were bare. Soon a coffee-bearer, the butcher's youngest son, appeared with a tray of small cups, and presently the eldest son of the butcher entered as pipe-bearer - a grave and solemn boy of fourteen, who first rested the bowl of the tchibouque at a measured distance on the floor, and then, on its axis, wheeled round the long tube, and gracefully presented it to Grigori on half-bended knee.

All the time, Grigori was aware of Olive Vanya Kharkov's unease, but a word by the butcher, and she was taken in hand by Madame Milosovic and spirited away to the recesses of the house. The men settled down to passing the tchibouque, the willing fume coming up, and tobacco glowing securely in the bowl.

From the top of the cart the executions had invigorated Karadan Milosovic. It always pleased him immensely when the Turks shot their own men rather than murdering Serbs. When the volley of shots had gone off, he had given a loud cheer in unison with the crowd. However, he thought, the little Muslim bitch had taken her time getting on the cart. She had not let the Russian help her up until after the volley had gone off. He was open enough to Grigori about it.

"She's a funny one her. I hate the pigs. They killed my brother and my first son."

Male or female, his hatred of Muslims ran deep.

"She's Ukrainian" Grigori told the butcher "and an Orthodox Christian."

Karadan Milosovic's face went red. "My apologies, friend."

The butcher beckoned to his eldest son who had positioned himself close by. He whispered in the boy's ear. The boy glanced quickly at Grigori, and then went quietly away to the back of the house.

"Once again, excuse me for speaking the way I did about your ......" He did not seem to have the right word to express what he was thinking. "I seem to have misjudged your whole situation. Forgive me."

Setting aside his patriotic and xenophobic beliefs, Karadan Milosovic was a good man. He was caught up in a nation's struggle for independence and Grigori could not fault him for his conviction. Any man, who was brave enough to hold to a cause, and fight for it, was to be respected. The whole of the Balkans was in potential turmoil, caught as it was between the three super powers of Austria, Russia and Turkey.

"The people have been subjugated and impoverish for too many centuries. We have nothing left to lose. We have designs for a Greater Serbia, a Serbia free of Muslims, with the Albanians, Bosnians, Macedonians and Croats under our sovereignty." Milosovic clenched his fist and brought it down on his knee.

"A Serbia for Serbs is one thing" interceded Grigori "but a Serbia intent on revenging centuries of wrongs, that is something that will lead to further conflict."

"So" said the butcher, sensing the difference of opinion and changing the subject "you want to go to Hungary?"

Grigori had no overwhelming desire to go to Hungary, but he had to pass through it to get to Vienna.

"Can you arrange it?" he enquired. "I have some papers."

"What about the girl?"

"The same." He was guessing that she wanted to come with him, for the look on her face had told him that she was a refugee who would go anywhere.

"The Austro-Hungarians distrust Russians, you'd have to be careful. I could get you Serbian papers and you could travel as man and wife." The statement shook Grigori. Man and wife? It was big step to take. He had no idea what sort of person the girl was; she might rob him at the first opportunity. But it could be useful for his purposes. "You could dump her in Budapest" Milosovic added.

Just as he was thinking about it, the butcher's wife appeared from the back of the house followed by the girl.

Grigori stared in disbelief. She was the most beautiful woman he had seen in his life. Until now he had only been aware of her eyes and hair, for she had quickly covered herself up again when he had put her back on her feet outside the fortress. He had spoken further with her in Russian as they had travelled to the butcher's house on the cart, and learned a little of how she had ended-up in Belgrade, but he had not thought of how she would have looked without her black Muslim clothing. Now, with the aid of Madame Milosovic, she had discarded the veil, and stood in the Milosovic's house dressed in a white bodice French dress that hugged her female contours and gave way to slender athletic legs tapering into a pair of fine Italian shoes. Even Karadan Milosovic gasped and remained speechless.

"Sir" spoke Madame Milosovic, addressing Grigori "I believe you are a gentleman. Take care of this girl. She has suffered unspeakable things." Madame Milosovic brought the girl forward and sat her down by Grigori's side. "Karadan, you must help her to get out of this country before someone further abuses her."

Madame Milosovic spoke as if she had seen something in the girl that either of the two men could see or imagine without seeing for themselves. Perhaps it was Madame Milosovic's motherly instincts, the experience of having lost one of her own sons. Perhaps it was something deeper, more to do with the intimate way in which women speak when they are alone. But whatever it was, Grigori felt that he would discover it by and by. Perhaps this well formed perfect being, sitting next to him without an outward blemish, had been scarred in brutal ways beneath her clothes, by those who had used her. He could only guess, but the intrigue fascinated him, and made him all the more ardent to discover more.

He spoke privately with her and discovered

that she was willing to travel with him to Vienna under the pretence of being his wife.

"If we are to arrange the papers, we must have names" said Karadan Milosovic. He took a pen and ink and a piece of paper from a drawer close at hand. "Now" he said jocularly "You are ...."

"Grigori Josef Shum, Count Rostov" said the Russian

The butcher looked at him disbelievingly. "Well, I suppose they might believe that" said the butcher for Olive Vanya's benefit writing it down "Vienna is full of imposters, believe me, I've been there on business to speak with Prince Alexander Karageorgvic. I may look like a humble meat-man, but my Serbian connections are excellent.

"Olive Vanya Shum nee Kharkov, Countess Rostov" said the butcher as he wrote. "And what is the profession of the Shum's?" asked the Serb. Without hesitation Grigori replied "Ballet master, and principal lady."

They all laughed, none totally believing the fiction they were creating, except for the new Count Rostov, a Russian man of greater experience and talent than anyone in that Belgrade room realised, but which in time, the new Countess Rostov would come to discover for herself.

"I'll have the papers ready by this evening" declared the butcher.

Madam Milosovic disappeared and re-appeared with a simple ring. She placed it on Olive Vanya's marriage finger of her left hand, and over a bible, solemnly pronounced that they were man and wife.

6

How is it, we may ask, that a man, or woman, driven by the events of history and war, left penniless and without property and connections, despite all, manages against all the odds to rise to a position of power and influence as if it is a god given right? You may say, yes, it is a man's ambition or a woman's determination to succeed that overcomes all the obstacles of place and influence that divides the truly great from those who never quite get started. That may be so, but there is also an element of fate, that chance of being in the right place at the right time, so that all other considerations are irrelevant, or at least minor to a freak of history.

Consider this - would the messenger who ran from Marathon with news of the Greek victory be remembered if it had been some other less worthy conflict? Would the love between Anthony and Cleopatra have been so great if Octavius had been a bad general? No, for it is impossible to have a great moment of human history without an even greater event to go with it. After the Battle of Waterloo, the Duke of Wellington was famous for beating Napoleon, but he was not Napoleon! Those who rise to greatest prominence too often plummet to the greatest tragedy. Yet, if they rise again, they rise with such swiftness of purpose and concentration that the whole world is in awe of their achievements.

So, it is with this in mind, we must now consider the life of Grigori, Count Rostov and his wife Olive Vanya as they approached Vienna. Olive Vanya's life, we may safely say, in her own way, had fallen, risen, fallen, and could only rise again, which it had already done so by meeting Grigori. The fluctuations had been minor on the larger scale of things - her vending into slavery, her elopement from Constantinople, Emil's capture - these were not events that shook the world, however traumatic or distressing they were for her. She knew nothing of politics, government or the ways of the ruling classes, in all these matters, she was as ignorant as the day she was born.

Not so with Grigori Rostov. Behind his steel blue eyes he could not hide the knowledge he had acquired as a privileged member of the Petersburg aristocracy. He knew the workings of the Russian imperial court intimately, and although, because of his years, he had never been called upon to advise anyone of any importance, never the less, he was at home in the claustrophobic atmosphere of an imperial court. It was with some irony that Karadan Milosovic had obtained papers for him that actually had reinstated him to his former rank, Count Rostov, for that is who he indeed was. However, it was still not clear to the Austrian authorities in the Hungarian frontier town of Semlin if he was a spy or a genuine refugee, and were it not for the possession of a letter of introduction to

Prince Alexander Karageorgvic of Serbia in Vienna, they would have detained him.

Throughout their journey through Hungary by Marie Thereasopol, Buda-Pest and Pressburg, the Count and his wife were thrown together in a situation in which neither knew how to react. The Count, an aristocratic gentleman at heart, when he discovered Olive Vanya, as she was now to be known, was only sixteen, he could no longer bring himself to think of her as a woman, and treated her like a child. This did not diminish his desire to bed her, for she was exquisitely beautiful, her only flaw being her youth.

The Count's failure to treat her like a woman dismayed Olive Vanya. She was already confused to find herself in another country where her language was not understood. The richness of the Hungarians also intimidated her, the opulence of the houses and gardens, which they saw as they travelled by public carriage the length of the country, made her reflect on how poor Turkey and Russia were by comparison. The roads were first class and without holes or dust, the people were clean and well fed and without plague, and the horses - of all the things she came at first to admire - it was the beauty of the Hungarian horses that most impressed her.

After awhile she was happy that Grigori had not made any advances on her. She felt that he was treating her kindly and that she must live up to the expectation of how a Countess should act. They both knew it was a sham, but it was convenient to them both. Olive resolved that until she had learned the language of the Austrians, she would speak nothing, and would only smile demurely if spoken to in Russian. She did not want to give away to anyone the fact that she was a peasant girl. She needed time to learn the ways of the aristocracy, and if silence was the only way that she could hide her ignorance and lack of grace, then she would live with that silence for years if need be. She had the greatest fear that if she were discovered to be an imposter, she would be sent back to Turkey, and the thought of that sent a shiver down her spine that made her sick.

She had experienced a similar feeling of sickness when Emil had touched her. Her body went cold, and she withdrew into herself to the extent that her muscles stiffened and her lips turned blue. That is how it had been with him. He had not tried to understand what had happened between her and her master Tapiq. She had been unable to tell him anyway - she could never find the words to express the horror she had endured in his bed.

However, for Olive Vanya, a more immediate fear was the realisation that Grigori might tire of her quickly if she could not amuse him, so to this end, throughout the journey she sang to him, and when they stopped, she made little plays and danced for him. She had learned such things in Constantinople, and she had seen how well they had pleased her master.

Grigori, for his part, could not believe the girl's talent. She was a natural entertainer.

In all his years in theatre and opera he had never come across such skills in one so young. He was excited, not by the coquettish movements and teasing of Olive Vanya or the songs of flirtation and love that she sang, but by the possibility of having found a star. All other matters aside, including his secret affairs of state (of which you will hear later), he felt that ahead in Vienna and Habsburg Austria lay a chance to remake his career in theatre and opera.

*

To understand the mighty power of Habsburg Austria, it is necessary to know something of its different people. Of its parts there was Austria which was truely German; Bohemia and Moravia, inhabited chiefly by Czechs, Slovaks and Germans; Hungary and its Maygars with Serb and Croat minorities; Galicia with its mainly Ruthenians and Poles; Transylvania with its Romanians of Latin stock; Illyria and Dalmatia with its Serbs and Croats; and Lombardy and Venetia, inhabited by Italians. Thus, Austria was a very diverse land, there was no overwhelming notion of nationhood binding its parts together. The government in Vienna permitted a wide variety of local difference, employing local officials instead of bureaucrats from Vienna. There was no attempt to Germanise or Austrianise the whole of the Empire, it was to all, an international empire.

However, the government in Vienna was inefficient, to the extent that the Emperor's government felt that it had sometimes ruled Europe, but had never governed Austria. When different parts of the Empire revolted, it was that which caused the trouble that became the solution of it - the existence of such a welter of different races. When in 1848 the Emperor Ferdinand had to abdicate in favour of Franz Josef, his son, on the surface, nothing had appeared to change. But out of the turmoil emerged a new Austria, an Austria which had ended the feudal privileges of the nobility, and freed the peasants from the bondage of serfdom.

*

The afternoon Grigori Josef and Olive Vanya arrived in Vienna was the same afternoon Sebastopol fell. Straightaway, with Olive Vanya placed in apartments in the house of the Countess Marie Festetics, Grigori called on Prince Alexander with his letter of introduction, and thereafter, things moved so fast, Olive had no notion of what was happening. During his absence, Olive had opened the large balcony windows of her bedroom and stepped on to the balcony. It was a glorious June afternoon, and there in the near distance were the blue waters of the Danube, the inspiration for the most famous waltz of the age. But the waters were not blue at that time of day, they were yellow-green, dyed by the meadows of cowslip and deposits of mud as the river meandered southwards for another thousand miles. The Viennese had not built houses along its banks as the Turks had done in Constantinople along the Bosphorous, the city had developed along the southernmost meander of the river, a useful waterway, far from the devastating floods of the main bed.

Olive watched fishermen bring their boats to the foot of a steep staircase which led down from the city ramparts, unload their cloth covered fish, and carry them into the fishmarket within the walls. Passengers from larger boats, not permitted on the narrow waterway, disembarked higher upstream and had to pass through the military cordons and city walls before reaching the main town. They crossed marshy meadows knee-high with glistening yellow globe-flowers, passing clumps of silver poplar heavy with rooks.

Olive's attention was suddenly brought back to focus, when from below the balcony on which she was standing, came a whistle. She looked down. There stood a blonde-haired young man at the door of Countess Festetics house, fresh faced, handsome, exquisitely dressed, with some books under his arm. She went to pull back from the edge of the balcony, but he said something.

"You are more beautiful than the Empress!" he shouted up with a smile.

Olive could understand a thing he was saying, but she remembered her promise of silence, smiled, and went inside.

A little while later she went back out on to the balcony, and the young man was back on the street accompanied by another young man. He shouted up again.

"See, this is my best friend, and even he

says you are more beautiful than the Empress."

Olive understood nothing. Momentarily in a panic, she thought that something was wrong, but the smile on the boy's face was evidence against such a conclusion, and once again she smiled back. They waved, she waved back, and they were gone.

Grigori returned solemn faced, but once he had a glass or two of Viennese wine, his spirits gathered. "I have to go away for a day or two" he spoke at last. The look Olive gave him was one of distrust and abandonment. He dug deep into his coat pocket. "Here" he said putting a large purse of florins into her hand "that will keep you going until I come back."

Olive was bewildered. As far as she knew, Grigori was penniless like herself. She did not know how much he had given her, but she knew it was a lot. She did not know how they had come to be in such a grand house as the Countess Festetics, it all seemed like a dream to her.

"Ask no questions" he said sternly. "Don't worry, I will be back in a few days" he said taking her face into his hands. "Enjoy yourself, Countess, this is Vienna!"

He spent an hour with her, suggesting how she might occupy herself in his absence. At one point he kissed her on the forehead like a father, and Olive threw her arms round him and cried. He told her not to be silly, and fearful that he might be cross with her, she wiped away her tears and asked if she could sing him a song. In his absence she had put some words to the Blue Danube tune, and she sang it to him with such sadness in Russian, Grigori's aloofness melted, and he kissed her again, this time on the lips, as a thank you.

As he was leaving, he consoled Olive Vanya "I have arranged for a tutor in German to visit you every day while I am away. His name is Grillparzer. It's said he's been a bit down on his luck since the Revolution, but I'm told he's the best." Grigori put a top-hat on to match the new suit he had purchased while he was out. "And, Olive, my dear" he spoke as a parting shot "I've arranged for Countess Festetics to take you shopping tomorrow for some new clothes."

7

Emperor Franz Josef was a dashing and accomplished dancer, and although, out of respect to this title, he did not dance at the formal Court balls and instead circulated in dutiful manner among the guests as was proper to his position, his mother Sophie arranged many highly exclusive informal parties for him of which he was the life and soul. Like any young monarch, he was surrounded by enchanting young countesses eager to please, and he enjoyed every minute of it, living for the moment like any other handsome young extrovert in his early twenties. Clean-shaven, the faint hint of Habsburg chin and lower lip did not distort, but rather, gave a cavalier edge to his youthful pink face. His hair was thick and slightly wavy, his cheeks had the well-fed look of aristocracy and went rather well with the bold, narrow blue eyes, that when studied, people thought too close together.

Yet, Franz Josef wanted very much to be married, and he had chosen his cousin Princess Anna of Prussia, a girl of his own age, elegant, slender, pretty, intelligent and sensible. She seemed to everyone in Austria to be the right sort of girl for Empress but she had snubbed him as she was in love with one of the Hesse-Kassels. His mother had pleaded with her sister Elizabeth, Queen of Prussia, to change the girl's mind, in fact she had thrown herself at her sister's feet in her plea for the marriage, but the political divisions between to the two nations were too deep, and her bowing's came to nothing.

Six months later, the Emperor's mother had gone to see another sister Ludovica, Duchess of Bavaria and invited her sister and two nieces to a family party at Ischl, in the lakes and mountains of Salzkammergut, the family's favourite retreat from Vienna.

Of the two sisters, Arch-Duchess Sophie had her eye on niece Helena, also twenty-two, presentable and handsome. If she had a reservation about Helena, it was that like her mother Ludovica, she was extremely religious. Sophie did not like the idea of the new Empress being open to exploitation by the Pope, for after a long struggle the Habsburgs had managed to wrestle the churches of their own empire from the control of the Vatican to the extent that the Pope's influence in Austria was almost negligible. She would have to keep an eye on her in this respect, but otherwise, to be religious gave a girl good morals and eliminated scandalous behaviour and any possible adultery.

However, at the informal ball at Ischl, Franz Josef could not believe his eyes. Helana was totally eclipsed by her sister Elizabeth. The sixteen year-old daughter of the Duke of Bavaria, tenderly known as Sisi, was the most beautiful woman in all of Europe! She had the finest forehead, with straight dark eyebrows over wonderful eyes, and extravagantly long and lustrous dark hair. Her face was an oval well set on a fine neck, her nose strong and straight if a shade too long. Only her mouth turned up at the corners, and this, with a chin that had that slightly unfinished look that goes so often with obstinacy of the passive kind, spoilt a picture of almost perfect natural grace and beauty.

Emperor Franz Josef had taken one look at his cousin Sisi and fallen. He became like a boy with a pet bird of many colours - he could not leave her alone. He doted every waken moment upon her and within forty-eight hours declared his choice to his mother.

The Arch-Duchess was disconcerted beyond measure. She raged at her son "Franzi! You fool! How can you fall in love with a sixteen year old girl who does not know a man from a horse?".

"It's Sisi, or nobody" shouted Franz Josef besides himself with rage, storming through the palace slamming doors.

"It is most unlike my son" said Sophie to her sister Ludovica, a faint and threadbare copy of Sophie herself.

"I don't think Elizabeth likes him all that much" Ludovica replied picking up her petticoats and letting them drop again. She smoothed out the satin material of her dress with the palms of her hands. "Helena is very upset" she muttered keeping her eyes fixed firmly on her hands.

"Oh, Vicky, it's a mess." Sophie, for the first time since the perils of the revolution, felt as though things had gone beyond her control. She stared at her sister on the chaise-long and wondered what sort of life she endured with her husband Maximilian, who Sophie had named her second son after. For her sister had all of Sophie's faults but none of her strength and had disappointed Maximilian by giving him five daughters, no sons. For years they had lived in seperate apartments at Possenhofen.

"Max dotes on Sisi" Ludovica added to the conversation "and Sisi dotes on Max. She cares nothing for me. She won't even go to mass with me."

"Nonsense, Vicky, nonsense" replied Sophie consolingly, but she knew it was true. Sisi could be a vindictive child if crossed. The thought of moulding her into an empress filled Sophie with dread. "When will you speak with her?"

"What?" Ludovica pushed her hands off her lap in an instant. "Are you serious? Elizabeth can't marry Franz Josef. She loves Possenhofen. She won't give up her horses for anybody."

*

"Do you love him?" Duchess Ludovica grilled her daughter. "For the sake of God, Elizabeth, I have to have this answer from you before we go home."

Sisi was crying. She was bewildered and did not really understand what the proposal meant. "How could anyone not love the Emperor?" She was very unhappy, but her mother could not understand whether she was unhappy about the Emperor wanting to marry her, or because she would have to give up everything in Bavaria and move to Vienna.

The truth of the matter was that she was far to young to be making any decision for herself as she did not know what she wanted. The thought of leaving Possenhofen made her feel so miserable, but the idea of marrying an Emperor filled her head with such dreams, she cried at that too. She kept asking herself 'Why me, of all the women in Europe, I am so young, so unimportant.' She could not really understand why the Emperor had fallen for her, he was more or less the first man she had ever met, and she certainly was not the first women the Emperor had kissed.

"Sisi" said her mother laying her hand around her shoulder "Do you love Franz Josef?"

"Yes, of course" said Sisi throwing off Duchess Ludovica's arm. "I do love the Emperor. But if only he were not the Emperor." She was fascinated by Franz Joseph, but at the same time in awe of him. "I shall do everything to make the Emperor happy" she added first believing it, then doubting it "but shall it be enough?"

"Well, I hope you know what you're doing, girl." With that, Duchess Ludovica went to find her sister Arch-Duchess Sophie to tell her that there was no objection to the marriage proposal of the Habsburgs from the House of Bavaria.

*

Like the rest of the Court, Arch-Duchess Sophie did not really know the character of her own son. They saw him as a likely kind of youth, good for mounting his horse and showing himself to his people. The rest of the world saw Franz Josef as a wonder youth who had been called to the appalling task of uniting Austria after the revolution and healing its internal ails. Yet, none were aware that Franz Josef was not appalled. Young, totally inexperienced, surrounded by the toughest advisors, and aware of the perils, he had taken the government of the nation in his stride without outwardly turning a hair. He was a man called by God. He was recalled to restore the fortunes of the divinely appointed House of Habsburg; to rule was his duty and right. As Emperor he saw the magnitude and difficulty of his task and his will was set firmly to meet it. He worked hard for at least ten hours a day, and nobody knew better than he how many ministerial proposals he sent back to be revised. Outwardly, his bearing was full of dignity, his behaviour to all exceedingly polite, though a little dry. Yet, until the appearance of Sisi, it had been said to

Arch-Duchess Sophie that her son had not much heart.

However, despite her aunt Sohie's interference in their relationship, Sisi had been attracted to Franzi, though at sixteen, she had not been ready for marriage of any kind. Apart from her liking of poetry and scribbling of verses, she had lived the carefree life of a boy rather than that of a girl. But married they were in the Augustinerkirche just outside the Hofburg, fourteen months before the arrival of the Count and Countess Rostov from Hungary.

8

When Olive Vanya Kharkov Shum, Countess Rostov arrived in Vienna, like the new Empress, she was still a child. Like the new Empress, she behaved like one, and by all of Vienna except her consort Grigori, Count Rostov, treated her like one. She was a moody, brooding, stubborn girl, yet nobody was more capable of flashing, dazzling gaiety when things were going well for her, or when she could do what she liked.

Olive Vanya, found her first difficulty had been coming to terms with the language - German. For Grigori, the task was a simple transition for he already spoke German fluently. In fact Grigori was the master of Russian, French, English and Italian, and street-wise in Arabic and some of the Slavic dialects. How and where he had learned these languages Olive did not know.

The arrival of Franz Grillparzer with a gentle knock at her apartment in the Festetic's house, and the look in the sardonic eyes of the sixty-four year old poet when he saw her for the first time, told her that he had been to both ends of life and come to rest somewhere in the middle through choice. He introduced himself with detachment and a voice that expected his name to be recognised, but which at the same time, intimated that the things spoken of him may have come from the lips of an enemy.

"Countess Rostov" he spoke in fluent Russian "this shall be the first and only time I will speak your language to you. From henceforth we shall speak only in German."

And so it was, and the daily lessons began, except for Sundays. At first, after the return of Grigori to Vienna, Olive had intimated that she did not want to continue with the lessons, but Grigori would not hear of it. Later, as her German improved and she began to converse in that fine language, she looked forward to Herr Grillparzer's daily visits. After three months, he became very dear to her, and he in turn, began to look on her like a grandchild. With the increase of her vocabulary came an increase of her knowledge of Austrian life and customs, but more importantly, through dear Franz, came a love for the German language.

Franz Grillparzer was no ordinary man. He was not like those writers who, once they reach a certain age and still find themselves in poverty, become bitter and twisted and see no merit in the works of others. He believed that life was a full circle and that his years of obscurity were part of that circle. He had grown up in a high, bare-room, sunless apartment at the very centre of the old town. His father was a lawyer, his mother a hyper-sensitive housewife, prone to melancholy, who ultimately committed suicide. There were occasional outings to the theatre, best of all to popular pantomimes. He had no liking for the church, and as a substitute he turned to music, encouraged by his uncle, Josef Sonnleithner, the writer of Fidelio. Then came the occupation of Vienna in '09 by Napoleon Bonaparte.

"My father was ruined by inflation, then sick, then died of a broken heart when the Emperor signed away Austrian sovereignty to the French."

"You must have felt awful" Olive Vanya declared in hesitant German, but using the correct past tense.

"I hated the French as much as my father, and yet Napoleon fascinated me with a magic power. I had never been addicted to military displays, and yet I did not miss one of his reviews of troops at Schonbrunn or Schmelz. I still see him before my eyes, running rather than walking down the open-air steps of Schonbrunn, behind him the Crown Princes of Bavaria and Wurtemberg, and then standing there cast-iron, hands folded behind his back to survey his troops with the unmoved look of lord and master. His figure is still present to me in my mind, but his features have merged with the many portraits I have seen of him since. He put me under a spell as a snake does a bird." Grillparzer looked out the window and down to the fishermen unloading their boats. "At night in the theatres the French cheered the music of Haydn, Mozart, and Beethoven, while outside, Vienna cried. And then came the new dawn. Prince Schwarzenberg defeated Napoleon at Leipzig. It was then that I truly began to write, as did Schubert and Strauss, and we created genius." Suddenly there was fire in his eyes, music in his ears, poetry on his lips.

"But what of love, Franz?" Olive questioned him, straining to understand every word he spoke in his soft Viennese way.

"I met Katty as she sat listening to Schubert playing the piano." Her name came from his throat as if so many years had passed since he last spoke it. "She was to marry my cousin Leopold Sonnleithner, Schubert's inseparable friend, and like him, now dead like him. She was not beautiful, but at twenty she was entrancing, her dark brown curls framing her mobile face which was dominated by dark, quick, expressive eyes. My, and how she had a hot temper, and a mischievous humour, but it was her independent spirit and frank tenderness that I liked most. And what a singing voice! She and her three sisters, singers all of them. Schubert valued her sister Anna's voice most highly and Josephine became a contralto on the operatic stage. Yet, I only had eyes for Katty. When I first saw her, she would not speak to me as she was too absorbed in Schubert's playing, but in the end she broke it off with Leopold, and we were engaged."

"Did you marry her, Franz?" Olive wanted to delve deeper, to know about love, to learn from the experience of others who had lived a life.

"No, but from that moment in Geymiller's music room in '21, Katharina Frohlich and I have been bound for thirty-four years. It has been an unbreakable relationship, frustrating, tempestuous, but totally satisfying."

"How wonderful" uttered Olive Vanya with a sincerity that pleased the old man.

"You, my dear" returned the old poet "your understanding of German is remarkable in this short time." He was genuinely impressed. He had known great men come to the city and not speak a word of the language after five years.

"Maester Grillparzer" Olive asked in a lower tone "Do you know someone who could teach me how to sing for the opera? Countess Festetics has found me a tutor called Herr Wagner but I don't think he is very good. He spends all his time making eyes at me."

"Leave it to me, dear." He smiled and took Olive Vanya into his frail arms. "A word of warning, my little dove - Vienna is beautiful, but dangerous too, for the pupil as well as the master. It's summer air saps strength, the hills and forest spread around you like magic land through which the blue waters glide. Music is all around, even in the trees when a choir of birds chorus up the dawn. It is easy not to speak, not to think, and take a half thought idea as the whole. And then there are the people, staunch of heart, healthy with commonsense who have covered up the truth with fairy tales and jokes. It is easy in Vienna to live in a half-poetry state without rhyme or stanza. It is full of beauty, and if we are not careful, we breathe but forget to exhale again the things we have hidden in our hearts. The artist's canvas stays empty."

His old man's lecture to a young girl over, he extended his arms, and held Olive Vanya by the shoulders. "Away, now, today you must go out, you must come to meet Katty!"

Before Olive could protest or excuse herself by saying she was waiting for Grigori to return, Franz Grillparser had handed her her parasol, closed the door of the Festetics behind them, walked her out on to the Ringstrasse, taken her down many side-streets and alleys, and into the world of the Biedermeier era in the Leoploldstadt district of the city.

*

Olive Vanya's second difficulty in Vienna had been her lack of social breeding and ignorance of basic etiquette. In this, Grigori taught her all, employing when necessary, tutors. Yet, in all matters, she was not ignorant, the household of her master in Constantinople had been a grand residence, and it had been the custom of the master, to teach the child he had bought in Russia how to read and write. It was with some pride that she looked back on her time in the Topiq household. Despite the horrific sexual favours she had to indulge her master with, he was kind and would have had her for his favourite if it were not for the severe jealousy of his other wives.

Olive Vanya's fatal mixture of extreme sensibility and extreme self-absorption had made her drawback into herself in Constantinople at the least rebuff from her master, or the lack of sympathy from his wives. With this went an unforgiving heart, for once Olive Vanya had taken against anybody she detested them for life, and her school-girl like hatreds persisted, unmitigated in Vienna. Only when the enemy was completely broken, as her lover, Emil, had been, or on the verge of death, as when Karadan Milosovic apologised to her in his sitting room in Belgrade, had she suddenly transformed into a radiant angel of forgiveness and consolation. Such moments were enough to create a legend, but were too infrequent and specialised to make her an easy companion.

Within months of arriving in Vienna, this strange creature from the Ukrainian peasantry found herself pitch forked into a world which was full of rebuffs and which showed no sympathy for her at all. From the chores and humiliations of Constantinople, she was plunged into the stiff, glittering un-ceremonial world of opera in Habsburg Austria, surrounded by men and women old enough to be her grandparents, most of whom had never been young.

Her co-tutees were strangers from other

lands, and they were presided over by the leathery-faced Anna Fruelich, who treated her from the start as a schoolgirl under instruction instead of a delicate young beauty called upon to sing. Franz had used his influence to get Olive Vanya into the class of 'dear' Anna's at the Philharmonic Society's conservatory. She was one of the grey eminences in Viennese musical life and everyone was terrified of her, but there was no doubting that she was the best teacher of singing in Vienna. The classes with Herr Wagner were discontinued, much to the distress of Richard Wagner, who had convinced himself, and her, and said as much, that he had fallen in love with her.

*

Olive Vanya's third problem was Countess Festetics, who had latched on to Count Grigori and had him very much to herself, and although jealous, Olive Vanya had been able to do very little about it.

How Grigori had come to know Marie Festetics was not clear to Olive. She had arrived home at the house the day after Grigori had left on business with Prince Alexander of Serbia, and she had spoken to Olive in charming Russian that gave way to probing questions about Olive's past.

The Countess Marie Festetics, cousin of Count Esterhazy, the Hungarian born Austrian Ambassador to the Vatican, looked about twenty five years of age, but was thirty-one, with a figure that men would find attractive, but which women would think of as skinny. She had a bony face and drawn in cheeks which were well powdered. Yet, her lips were truly beautiful, full, rounded, and not at all cruel like her green eyes which when brought to bear upon Olive, bore right into her. Her face fixed itself into an expression that Olive did not like, the sort of expression that told Olive that Marie Festetics knew something which she should not have known.

"This will never do! Grigori has been awful to you. Look at this dress you are wearing." She had felt the hem of Olive's dress and let it drop in disgust. Grigori had bought her the dress in Buda-Pest.

True to herself, Olive remained tight lipped and pretended not to understand the Countess's continuous questions. All the time, the Countess circling her, had looked her up and down with a sound of tut-tut emitting from her lips.

The Countess's house was an enormous Baroque edifice in the Singerstrasse with a plain front and two receding wings, its doorway flanked by two pairs of muscular Atlantean figures. Inside there was a great hall at the foot of a marble staircase, but there were no staterooms, and in all, with its four separate apartments, the front of the house promised far more than its interior fulfilled.

There was no Count Festetics, he had since passed away from an unexplained illness. There was only a younger brother of the Countess, Stepan, who by all appearances and by the accounts of his sister was a wastrel. He was the young man that Olive had seen from the balcony, but not the one with the blonde hair. That had been Ferdinand Maximillan, the brother of the Emperor Franz Josef.

To return to Olive Vanya, she was curious as to how the Countess had met Grigori, and she listened for clues whenever his name was mentioned, for Marie Festetics was a woman who could not keep quiet.

"The Count Rostov is a very fine man, a very fine man" she repeated. They were shopping for dresses, hats, gloves, parasols, shoes, under-garments, capes, canes, jewellery, perfume, make-up, handkerchiefs, opera glasses - in fact, everything that the young Countess Rostov would need to enter Viennese society. "We have everything in Vienna, better than you would ever find in Petersburg."

'So,' thought Olive Vanya 'she's been to Saint Petersburg.'

"Don't you ever say anything, kind" she said exasperatedly in one shop "I don't believe Grigori when he says you can sing. You can't even talk." She laughed, but it was not a cruel laugh, her beautiful mouth did not have a twist, it was a laugh at the situation, at having to choose everything for a teenage girl who complained about nothing.

Marie Festetics, in spite of herself, liked the girl. It did not seem to matter what she said to her, she returned a pleasant smile. She knew the girl could understand everything she said to her, that she was keeping up the pretence of being the Countess Rostov admirably, that perhaps, given time, she might actually get away with convincing people that she was an aristocratic girl with very little to say. But for the sake of Marie's relationship with Grigori, and her relatives who were in the government, the little peasant girl wife made the comings and goings of Grigori at all hours of the night, respectable.

However, what worried the Countess Marie about the girl was - that no matter what clothes she tried on, she looked radiant. Everything suited her, even when down to her underwear, she looked like a little Greek goddess. More than once, Marie caught herself looking in the mirrors of the salons to see if in fact she herself had grown old, and it concerned her, that ultimately, Grigori might prefer this slip of a girl to herself.

9

None of the events that overtook Grigori Josef Shum, Count Rostov, were without design. He was a spy. From the age of eighteen he had been employed by the internal affairs ministry of Csar Nicholas in the art of espionage. In this field of service he had been trained in Russian theatre and opera with instructions to report subversion wherever he found it. He had been partly responsible for sending Lermantov and Dostoevsky on the long march to Siberia and had come close to recommending the same fate for composers Glinka and Dargomijsky. With the outbreak of the war in the Crimea, he had been dispatched by the foreign affairs ministry   to Sebastopol to assess morale. A month later, he was informed that he was to travel incognito to the Balkans to assess the feelings of Russian sympathisers who wished to throw over Ottoman rule.

During his year in the Balkans (travelling with his dancing bear), Grigori had made contact with the revolutionary forces of Rumania and Wallachia, promising them Russian arms when they were ready to overthrow the Turks. In Belgrade, before the day of the firing squad outside the fortress, he had already made contact with the Karageorgists and Karadan Milosovic; his journey on to Vienna had been planned in advance, for as well as helping the Karageorgists, Grigori Josef had been instructed by Petersburg to infiltrate the government circles of Vienna as their regular agent had been discovered and secretly executed by the Austrians.

The one thing that had not been well planned was Olive Vanya. Grigori had used the girl to get himself into Austria, but it had been his intention to get rid of her quietly the night before he reached Vienna. He was well trained in assassination, but somehow, he could not bring himself to kill the girl. In her, he saw something that served his ambition.

All his adult life, Rostov had harboured a dream. He had been trained by the government to direct plays and operas, yet in all that time, touring the theatres of Russia, spying for the Csar, he had never been happy with his productions. Anyone of genius hid that genius under a bushel, for if genius shone too bright in Csarist Russia, it was extinguished by exile in Siberia. He, in his own way, had been responsible for the censorship of ideas and the destruction of genius in his own productions.

Now, here in a peasant girl, singing to him, playing out scenes before him, he saw the genius that had been missing from all his theatre work. Sitting, watching her, he imagined the Opera House in Vienna full of the richest people in Austria, the Emperor and Empress, the music of Mozart or Beethoven, a corps de ballet, the voice and writing of Nestroi, and the soprano of this common, serf of a girl, who looked like an angel.

He saw it all, there before him as she entertained and toyed with him, teased and sung to him with such a voice that he was besides himself with joy at her discovery. He had to do it! He had to take the risk of keeping this girl, not for his lover, far from it, but as his dream. She would need training, she would need clothes, she would need everything that every other woman in Vienna had, and he would find a way. His Russian masters would pay him handsomely for the Vienna post. The Karageorgists would pay him for his services. But above all, Marie Festetics would help him most with introductions and connections. It would be a long and painful rise to the top for his protégé; it would add a risk to his Vienna assignment; but he would instruct this girl well, and make a countess out of a peasant.

*

Olive expected that Marie had discovered the truth about the Count and her and used it over him whenever they argued about her that they frequently did when he came to the house, but she was wrong in this. Grigori had told Marie nothing about Olive Vanya except what she found out for herself. Grigori had made up a story, which Olive Vanya stuck to, that Grigori had met her in Sebastopol, that her family had been ruined by the war, that the English had killed her parents, and that Grigori had married her in order to get her out of Russia. They were not lovers; she, Olive, was his pupil, who he had brought to Vienna to train as an opera star.

Whenever Olive Vanya woke in the night to hear Grigori and Marie arguing, at first it made her cower. Later, she thought they really hated each other and were going to kill each other, and she would pull herself out of bed to see what was going on, only to catch glimpses of them frolicking on the sofa in Marie's apartment. Embarrassed she would always flee back to her own bed, but as time went on, she became angrier, and more jealous. One night she awoke to find Marie dragging her out of the bed and across the floor and shouting at Grigori "to get the little bitch out of my house!", but Grigori had saved her, put her back to bed, and in the morning Marie had apologised and said it would not happen again. But it did, frequently, not always in the same way, but with the same end.

After awhile, Olive Vanya started to suspect

that it was Grigori who held something over Marie, and not the other way around. He came less and less often to the house and laid down more and more rules about the tuition of Olive Vanya. He told Marie that Olive had to be approached with circumspection, that she was to be smothered, that she was not to be allowed too much freedom during his absences, and above all, she was to be kept away from dilettantes and philanderers.

Nothing should have been easier for these two intriguers, Grigori and the Countess Festetics, than to make Olive go their way, for she was an angelic singer, and all Vienna talked about her performances. But nothing in fact was more difficult; the child star would not be led; she showed vice, and bit, and kicked when they tried to bridle her. She was, when all was said, a Russian peasant girl, and to this irrefutable fact she clung, even when, within weeks of her first soprano role, she was weeping her heart out to Grigori, still very much in league with Countess Festetics , and pouring out her soul in adolescent verses she showed to Franz Grillparser - sustained paradoxes of homesickness and revulsion.

*

Grigori, in his infrequent returns to Vienna, was in a wienstube facing the University reading a newspaper and sipping wine. Outside towered the ramparts of the old city walls. When he looked up, he could see from his seat at the window the Pasqualati House in which Beethoven had lived some years before. From the windows of these rooms could be seen the Wienerwald Hills with their vineyards. Where Grigori was sitting he could not see the hills or anything on the other side of the thick walls, but two hundred years before, this particular rampart had been the target of fierce attacks by the besieging Turks.

Nestroy walked in. He immediately saw the Count sitting at the window half-hidden by that day's newspaper. He greeted him cordially, and the Count ever eager to meet new friends as if they were old, rose to his feet, took the actor's hand, and kissed him on both cheeks.

"Johann, come sit." Grigori ushered Nestroy, the most famous actor-singer in Vienna before the turmoil, into a seat. As they waited for their light-lunches to arrive, Johann Nestroy produced a manuscript from the skirts of his coat.

"No, Johann, I only want you to sing in my opera, not write it."

"Read it, Grigori Josef."

"The Old Man with the Young Wife" read Grigori out loud "Is it a comedy?"

"I wrote it just after the Revolution. It's a popular play for the people about a well-to-do manufacturer called Kern."

"It's a farce, then?" asked Grigori.

"No! It's about the escape of a political prisoner. See, Count, because of our short intoxication with freedom after the Revolution, many political offenders were sentenced to ten or fifteen years in prison. In my play none of these heroes lose honour for even quarter of an hour. The respect the play gives to every man who sticks up for his opinion, risks his life for his faith ... that respect is his forever ..."

"Yes, Johann, but is there a place for singing in the piece? I've got to be able to get people into the opera house."

"Count .... what my hero did before he was imprisoned, was done by hundreds of thousands, by nearly everybody in Vienna - no matter if it was by deed, word or thought - Revolution was in the air, everyone breathed it in, so that what he breathed out again had to be Revolution. It is just that one person or another attracted more attention than another. See, in this play, I'm trying to heal Austria's wounds. All I'm saying in the play is .... even if you have been imprisoned, don't condemn your judges. After a revolution, there is no such thing as a right measure of punishment. According to the law, hundreds of thousands deserve death - but that's impossible to carry out. So one man is shot 'for life', the next gets fifteen years in jail, this one gets six weeks, that one gets a fine, and another ends up a Count. And at same time they've all done the same thing." Nestroy was waving his hands around as if he was downstage and the footlight candles were in his face.

"You'll never be able to get a license for a play like this, Johann." Grigori was reading some of the text and shaking his head. "Nobody will ..... it won't get past the censors."

Johann spat on the floor. "I tell you, Grigori Josef, even in Russia there must be greater artistic freedom than this. Here in Vienna the spirit is getting worse every day, but we are too cunning to let it come to an armed showdown with the Emperor's army."

"The Revolution failed you, Johann, as all revolutions fail the people. There will always be revolutions, and after the revolutions there will always be kings, queens, emperors, presidents, dictators, call them what you may. Revolutions don't change anything?"

There was no mistaking that Nestroy was whole-heartedly a partisan of the democratic movement in Vienna. Grigori had admiration for him, for at the height of mass excitement of '48 which saw street barricades, revolutions, and falls of government right across Europe, Nestroy's Freiheit in Krahwinkel in the Leopoldstadter had played daily to over-full houses. Now, Nestroy was playing on his past glories, and Grigori, looking for a commercial success, wanted the hero of '48 to give up writing and go back to singing.

"Johann, politics can be the death of any man's career. Having lived under the regime of a despot, I know. I was banished to Sebastopol to work with an opera company I'd never heard of. When I arrived there, I found I'd been given charge of a misfit group of exotic dancers to entertain the fleet. As if this were not enough to crush me, the French and English began bombarding Sebastopol. To my mixed fortune, a night of serious bombardment destroyed the performance hall and most of my dancers were killed or maimed. I suddenly found myself with no cast, no theatre, and absolutely no reason to remain in Sebastopol in the middle of a war. So I fled."

Grigori paused. He was trying to make a point to Johann Nestroy, but it was taking rather longer than he expected. "The short of it is this, Johann. I did not fall into disfavour in Petersburg because I dared to criticise the Csar." Grigori paused for a sip of wine. "No, Johann, my crime was to be in possession of a copy of Thomas Paine's Rights of Man. If it had been Marx's Das Kapital I would have been sent to Siberia."

Johann Nestroy stared blankly in disbelief. "You were sent to the Crimea for possessing a book?"

Grigori handed him back the script. He knew to take on The Old Man and the Young Wife would be artistic suicide for him in Vienna. Over the past two years he had worked hard to ingratiate himself with the ruling classes and find favour with the businessmen of the day, the ones who put the money into productions. He was not going to jeopardise that for anything. The memories of travelling with the bear to avoid detection were still vivid. He liked his posting in Vienna.

Johann nodded and seemed to accept Grigori's refusal to look at his play with a resignation that was inbuilt from years of struggle. Much of the rest of their lunch was spent in idle gossip about acquaintances, the weather, and singing. Johann rose.

"Thank you, Grigori Josef. I think I'll go

back to my first love now."

"I didn't know you were married, Johann?"

"Acting, my dear Count" he said with the flair of a man always possible to bounce back from rebuff. "My first and only love. The revolution was my greatest role. But now, Grigori Josef, if you ever need a tenor to sing opposite your sweet little Countess, count me in."

With that final play of words, the great Johann Nestroy shook the Count's hand, embraced him in farewell, and without a backward glance, left the smoke filled wienstube.

Grigori settled down to his newspaper once more, reflecting that he may have been too hard on the actor, but he genuinely felt, lies aside, that amongst honest men, honesty held more terrors than the bullets of a revolution, and that the production of subversive work in Vienna, was against the interests of Russia as well as his own.

10

The city of Vienna was not as Olive had imagined it. Initially it had enthralled and vexed her all at the same time. Now, she was tiring of it. She was in love with Grigori and she couldn't bear it any more.

Then, Olive found one ally in the Court - Sisi, the Empress Elizabeth. It was almost as if they were thrown together by everyone-else's manoeuvrings and envies. For while Empress Elizabeth's beauty, indeed, aroused the enthusiasm of the common people who saw her, she struck jealousy into the hearts of those who mattered at the Court of Vienna. Likewise, Olive Vanya, appearing from nowhere as a sixteen year old singer, had advanced to the pinnacle of Viennese opera in a space of four years, an unparallel rise, and one that, if many jealous of her had their way, would end soon.

Both Sisi and Olive were foreigner's in the Austria, both were beauties that far outshone any of the other women in Vienna; both were treated with contempt and disrespect. Morning to night there was no privacy for either. From the moment the young Empress emerged from her bedroom, dressed for public appearance, she was on view to the moment she went to bed. Likewise, Olive, adored by men wishing to gain her favour, could virtually not move in Vienna without an entourage of protection organised by Countess Marie Festetics and her close friend, Frau Ida von Ferenczy, who kept an eye on her more-or-less from the moment she rose, to the moment she went to bed.

Sisi wanted nothing more than to be with her husband, and when she could not be with him, she wanted to be alone, preferable at Laxenburg, a small but delightful palace in the country just outside Vienna. Olive wanted nothing more than to be with Grigori, her husband, but when she could not, and that was more and more frequently, she would take her horse, which she had duly been taught by Grigori to ride, and canter to the country along the road to Hungary.

Olive enjoyed riding, it was her one opportunity to escape the Countess and Frau Ferenczy, both city ladies, who could not ride at all. On her rides Olive would regularly pass the palace of Laxenburg with its beautiful park laid out in on English lines and marvel at the fine horses stabled there. It was well known that the Empress, under the watchful eye of the twisted old Arch-Duchess was slowly becoming a prisoner at Laxenburg, a victim of the Habsburg dynasty.

Then, by chance very early one spring morning near the gates of Laxenburg, Olive encountered the Empress Sisi out riding alone with her dogs, and for some reason which became plain to her later, Sisi came up to her on her mount at a full trot.

"Good morning!" she exclaimed without pretension or condescension "I cannot bear to let this beautiful morning pass without sharing it with someone. Have you seen the blossom, it is everywhere. It is like the whole world is snowing blossom."

It was one of those rare moments in life when nature displays to mere mortals the wonder of creation. The whole of Laxenburg Park was in bloom, not just the hedgerows, or floral beds, or the cherry trees - but the whole of the park was a whirl of fallen blossom - pinks, reds, white, yellows. It was magic, as if the world was raining confetti and the whole of mankind was asleep and missing one of the miracles of creation.

The Empress, without ordering or expecting refusal, turned her mount. Olive was in a trance, as if she had been hypnotised by the scent of the fallen blossom.

"Come on" the Empress said to her again in a coaxing manner as she sped into a cantor and dropped low on her mare to avoid low hanging branches. Olive, a good horsewoman, but less able, somehow managed to follow the Empress in and out of the trees and on over the velveteen to the gates of Laxenburg and into the most splendid paradise she had ever been in her whole life. She followed on as the Empress wound in and out the orchard trees letting the blossom cover herself and the horse and the following dogs until she reined to a halt beneath a chestnut tree grove that towered and arched above them like a Roman Arch. The ground was so thick with white flower petals the dogs began to sneeze. The Empress, circled by her dogs, began playing with them, rolling in the petals like a child, laughing, giggling, forgetting who she was. Olive dismounted, and set upon by one of the small dogs, likewise began to roll in the petals, until like the empress she was buried by blossom. The dogs went quiet, and the two most beautiful women in Austria lay there, some meters apart, staring up into the blizzard of blossom falling on them from above.

11

Grigori came to see Olive Vanya when he knew that Marie was at the wedding engagement party of Prince Maxmillan who had also invited Olive, by way of Stepan, to the party, but Grigori had ordered Marie not to let her go. The Prince had too many young friends and Olive Vanya's head might have been turned by one of them. Sisi had also wanted her to come to the Hofburg, for she had become concerned that Olive's life was being wasted by the notoriously secretive Count Rostov.

The visit of Grigori took Olive by surprise, for it had been a long time since Grigori had come specifically to see her without first having to get past Marie.

"Grigori" panted Olive "what are you doing here?"

"To talk" said Grigori. "How are you?" It had been two months since he had last spoken to her.

"Fine, a little tired from all the singing."

He took her by the waist and lifted her up the way he had first done when they had met at the executions in Belgrade.

"You've put on weight." He slowly lowered her, and as her face came level with his own, he kissed her.

Olive did not resist as he kissed her again. She did not know what was on his mind, but she put her arms around his neck as they sank on to her bed. He began to remove her clothing and she lay there and let him do so. He removed his own clothes without a word and began making love to her. Suddenly, as if some great guilt had descended on him, he halted. He dressed again, and immediately drank some wine.

Why, Olive asked herself, why had he waited four years to do that, then stopped? Why?

"Grigori?"

Grigori was silent and morose. The blood had drained from his face the same way it had done on that first day in Vienna after he had been to see Prince Alexander Karageorge, now king of Serbia.

"I'm in trouble, Vanya" he trembled taking another glass of wine "I have to go away."

"But you are always going away" replied Olive "what's so different this time?"

"I won't be coming back. My time here is over."

"What do you mean? Your whole life is here. We have another production coming up at the Opera House. We've got Johann Nestroy and Giuseppe Mario for the men, I'm singing with Wilhelmine Schroder, Richard Wagner's writing the music, and we've got the Philharmonic Orchestra. You can't leave now?"

"All that will go on. There's none in Vienna can match your singing, not Clara Novello, not anybody. I'm proud of you, you don't know how proud of you I am."

"Grigori, I don't care about the singing." It was true, she had long given up caring about her singing, it was not enough to live a life for. "It's you Grigori that I care for. I always have, since the moment I met you."

Naked, but unashamed, she crossed the room, knelt by his side, and laid her head in his lap. He did not stir, it was as if some great brooding had overtaken him, and he could not shake the darkness of it off.

"Get up, Vanya, don't look at me with those big brown eyes, please. I've given you everything I have, I can't give you anymore."

"I don't want anymore, all I want is you, my husband."

Grigori sprang to his feet and crossed the room. "You are not my wife, Vanya, we were never married. It's all a sham, a make-believe, can't you see that. You are just my dream, my fantasy. Every man has to have a dream, an escape from this awful world we call life. Don't you think that I love you? I have never loved anything so much in my life, but I know I can't have you, because I will destroy you with my lying, my cheating, my vile temper. You know nothing about me. I am not an opera director. I am a spy! A Russian spy! Do you hear me. I've even using Marie to get information about the Austrian government in return for helping her cousin Esterhazy plan for Hungarian separation. I'm playing a dangerous game and I'm cracking up! I have to go away."

Olive shivered on the polished floor of the bedroom. She began to cry.

"I've used you too, Vanya, I've used you most of all. I've destroyed the innocent peasant girl and created another aristocrat. If only I had left you as you were." He picked her up off the floor. She tried to struggle, but he was too strong for her. "Remember this. I am not all bad. I will send you money and you can find you own apartments in Vienna so that you can carry on singing." He wrapped her in a blanket. "But from now on, you must make your own way in the world. I will always think of you as my dream. So, before I go, I want you to sing one last song for me, the one you wrote to the tune of the Blue Danube our first day here, remember? Come, then " he led her to the window and threw it open to the night. "Sing."

The feelings of four years ago came flooding back to Olive as she saw the Danube in the near distance. To the south, small puffs of clouds were gathering, with the sweet colour only spring can give; the metal roofs of the town shone and shimmered in the moonlight, and at times a distant flock of pigeons cut white wheeling curves into the blue river.

*

That night after Grigori had gone, Olive chose to climb one of Vienna's western hills, and saw the dawn rise over the big town - first a a faint strip of light unfolding in the east, white fogs glimmering along the Danube, then the town lifting out of the night haze in massed bulk, partly set aflame, partly still struggling with a sombre golden, billowing smoke from chimneys, the whole prospect strewn with gold stars that sparkled from windows, roofs, steeples, lightning rods, while out on the horizon, a pale green ribbon of country gently grew large across the sky. From the wood-clad ridge to her left came no shade yet, only a mild breathe of air that had been asleep among the leaves. On the right, a green slope on which she climbed the previous night, descended to the long furrow of the valley where the roofs began and glinted through the treetops. Behind garden fences, vineyards and arable land gave out to pasture and the quarries from which Vienna was built. The rest was blocked by meadows and wooded knolls, the town wedged between the river and the hills.

Olive Vanya did not move all day. She waited until there were no more tears, and returned to the city after nightfall came.

12

A military ball had been arranged at the Hofburg prior to the departure of the Emperor's armies to fight the Piedmontese in Italy. The French Emperor Napoleon III had sprung to the aid of Victor Emanuel and supplied the Piedmontese with a stockpile of arms. The Emperor's government, impatient as always, had demanded that the Piedmontese should disarm, but the Piedmontese, forever with a desire to unite Italy, had flatly refused. It was their intention to chase the Austrians out of Lombady, Venetia, and Italy for good. Austria, now appearing to be the aggressor, had declared war .

The faces of the army officers were gay, but the mood of the evening was sombre. There was a foreboding that Austria would lose Lombardy and the rich farmlands of the Po. The prosperity of the area was great, and it had benefited directly from Austrian irrigation schemes, and the Austrians had not easily moved the peasants and artisans to hatred. It was from the nobility and the intelligentsia that the most stubborn opposition came. The

Empress was unforgiving of them.

"Three winters ago" continued Sisi to her new confident, Olive Vanya, who was now seen frequently at Court events "I went with Franzi on a tour of Venetia and Lombardy. It was Buol's idea, that obstinate little man over there." She drew Olive's attention to the Foreign Minister, a small, cold looking man with arrogant manners "He is like a locomotive who does not know where it is going, and when asked, answers only with steam and whistling."

The Count Ferdinand Buol-Schauenstein had been at the thick of the negotiations with the Piedmontese and had inadvertently made a regional conflict into a European war. With the French backing the Piedmontese, Buol had tried to drag the Prussians and English into the conflict as Austria's allies. He had failed miserably, and from the reaction of the military commanders about him that evening, he knew they despised him, for the Austrians had now to take on the French and Piedmontese alone. Not one man at the ball relished the prospect.

"That horrible little man will be quietly dismissed by Franzi tonight" Sisi said venomously. "I can never forgive him for what happened in Italy. First in Venice, then in Milan, the streets and squares were crowded with our Italian subjects. Franzi looked like the most handsome young emperor there had ever been. We were head over heels in love. The army and the police were ready to cope with any trouble but we expected none as Franzi had granted amnesties to all political prisoners. But ..."

She paused. There was a slight tear in her eye as if she had been wounded by the prick of a rose. She bit the edge of her fan.

"I can never forget the silence of the people as went about in our open carriage, no amount of army or police could do anything about the utter silence. The vast crowds who saw us everywhere just gazed. The brilliant receptions that that been arranged were boycotted by the leading Italian families, and those who did turn up had to face crowds of hissers. In Venice, before the visit was over, the crowds began to soften, and Franzi told me that was because they could no longer go on hating me because I was so beautiful."

Sisi sighed a sigh that only those who have experienced such things can fully understand.

"But, the nobility still stayed away. Everywhere we went it was the same. Milan was worse than Venice. There was a gala night at La Scala. Radetzky and Buol were determined to fill the vast auditorium, for they feared that half the boxes would be empty. So Buol demanded in advance to be informed by subscribers whether they proposed to be present or not, and if not, unused boxes were to be filled by Austrian officials and their wives, duly dressed for the occasion."

Olive Vanya was curious about La Scala "What was the opera, Sisi?" she asked quickly as if not trying to disturb the

Empress's concentration.

"Verdi's Rigoletto" she replied gravely "They could not have picked a darker story if they had tried. If this is the sort of opera that Austrian occupation inspires, then let them go their own way, that's what I told Franzi. But, no, he shrugged it off, but even he could not shrug off the snub of the great families who said they would come but did not - instead they sent their servants. Their servants ..." she repeated as if the experience of sitting in the royal box of the great opera house of Milan surrounded by servants who had shown hatred she had never before encountered. It had un-nerved her. "The easy going, laughter-loving Italians hated everything I stood for, though I had done nothing wrong. They hated the Emperor and his entire Court, they hated Austria." She took a sharp intake of breath as though someone had put a knife between her ribs, then bit her lip.

"It affected Franzi deeply" the Empress continued. "He talked about it for weeks. When we got home he had Radetzky resign. He had decided to put in place in Italy a benevolent civilian rule instead of a military dictatorship. He gave Max the job as Governor-General."

Olive Vanya saw the Emperor's younger brother waltzing about the dance-floor like a mad-man. According to gossip, Franz Josef and Ferdinand Maximillan had always got on well together.

Max had changed since that first time Olive had seen him in the street with Stepan. He was still tall, dreamily handsome with silky blonde hair, but his student days had turned him into a poetic dreamer. Sisi liked him immensely and had introduced Olive to him on a number of occasions, but Olive was wary of him, for his eyes were not the eyes of four years before. In them she now saw the look of the dilettante, a man jealous of his brother. Max knew he was more popular than his cold, aloof brother, whose nature he did not understand. Maximillan knew he was destined for greater things. He knew his brother had sent him to Milan to cut him down to size, but he had not succeeded. He was back at court with his new wife Charlotte, daughter of King Leopold of Belgium, and he was delirious with happiness about his new, beautiful, highly-strung, intelligent, witty mate.

The timing of the marriage could not have upset Franz Josef more. Max had made a mess of Italy, but instead of returning to Vienna for forgiveness, he had contemptuously married Leopold's daughter at a time when Austria was trying to make friends with France. It was well known that Napoleon III wished to incorporate the newly created Belgium into the French Empire, but the marriage of the Emperor of Austria's brother to the King of Belgium's daughter, indicated to Napoleon that Franz Josef was sending him a warning.

Maximillan did not care. He would do as he pleased. He would not be like his brother - acting like a God, issuing divine orders to mortals. He had a joie d' vive that he would not suppress for the sake of his brother and Austria. He loved Charlotte, and she was his wife. However, what he could not see, but what many at the court could perceive in Charlotte, was that she was a self-dramatist who made scenes to curry attention, and who, when all was said and done, was devoured by ambition, and envious of her sister-in-law Sisi, Empress of Austria, as much as Max was of the Emperor. Her jealousy also appeared to extend to anyone close to Sisi.

"Dear, Charlotte" Sisi smiled taking the hand of her in-law "this is the Countess Rostov, Vienna's theatrical jewel." Sisi took Olive's hand and placed it beneath her sister-in-law's. Olive curtsied.

"Levez-vous" Princess Charlotte said speaking down the bridge of her nose in a condescending tone "You speak French?" she asked in stilted German.

"No, highness, not well." Olive had been instructed in French at Grigori's insistence, but she had firmly resisted the lessons, much to the dismay of her tutor.

"Not the language of the moment" interrupted the Empress "especially when we are about to go to war with them."

Princess Charlotte took offence. "Wars never last, but great languages go on forever. It appals me that the Emperor's court does not conduct it's social business in the only language fit for empires. Even the Csar of Russia insisted on speaking French when I was there." Charlotte's voice rose sharply as if she was trying to make a scene. She stared haughtily up into the air, no doubt with the purpose of composing her next condescending remark. A number of officers and their wives stared at her, the desired affect of her actions. Prince Maximillan, totally unaware of what had gone before, came whirling off the dance-floor, and interrupted.

"Come on, Charlie." He grabbed his petite Belgian wife by the wrist and spirited her away on to the ballroom floor before she could lower her nose and utter another word.

Sisi turned with a smile on her face, then buried her head behind her lace fan, and sniggered. It was not empress-like, but Olive, no better at hiding her emotions in public, openly laughed at the conceitedness of the new court addition. From across the room, Franz Josef caught the laugh and waved to them as he tried to disengage himself from a conversation with Buol.

"I tell you, sire, Malmesbury does not want Italy to be united. The Queen of England doesn't want it. If Napoleon makes war on us, they believe Prussia will support us, then Belgium, and so drag England into the confrontation as Belgium's ally. It will be 1815 all over again, and France will the crushed."

"Buol, you fool, Prussia wants us weakened ...." The Emperor gave up. He had taken Metternich's recommendation that Buol was an able man, and now it had cost Austria its alliance with Russia, the German states, and brought them to war with France. "Sir, you are relieved of your duties. And I will hear no more about it." The generals attending the Emperor confirmed the finality of the Emperor's statement. Count Buol, publicly humiliated, departed unceremoniously, accompanied from the Hofburg by an attaché and military escort.

The ball continued as the business of the court was dispensed by the Emperor.

"Physically and morally" continued Sisi *tete a tete* with Olive, and becoming bored with the evening "Franzi is fearless, and I believe the main reason he can face the truth, however bitter, is that it does not frighten him. It is said that time will make him more self-reliant; I do my best to assist that good work; but this country has him as a husband, not I."

Olive studied the Emperor as if she were at the theatre and watching a play. He was dressed in an all white military style tunic with gold epaulettes, a red and gold sash across his right shoulder, red breeches with gold piping, a sabre in a gold scabbard on his left hip. His chest was decorated with the orders of the Empire - a blaze of gold, rubies, and diamonds.

Olive could not decide if he were a comedy or tragedy, for the elements of the picture presented before her could not be fitted into a single opera. He was a man whose whole life was the Empire, and here before him at the ball, were the most dazzling array of military men, their wives and daughters. The splendour of the Austrian army was undoubtedly the finest in Europe.

"Note, dear Olive" whispered Sisi in her ear as they watched the Emperor tour the fringes of the ballroom "that he is not superficial. He is always sincere and hates any kind of lie. He is very discreet, but what I cherish most, is his courage. I have never seen it fail, even in the most difficult situations."

The Emperor was talking to Field-Marshal Gyulai, commander-in-chief of the imperial army. He was no ball of fire. He was a man of monumental crassness, blessed with the calm that so often goes with stupidity, a man who had no wish to be commander-in-chief. He told the Emperor's Adjutant-General so, but the Emperor dismissed his lack of nerve for modesty. He spoke frankly with Gyulai

"We had taken for granted that Prussia would help us."

"Sire, I reported to Buol that the regime of the army was deplorable. My quartermasters are corrupt and inefficient, the conscripts ill-trained, the field officers under my command owe their rank to birth and wealth, while my company officers are totally underpaid." Gyulai took in a deep breath, he did not want the command, but he could not refuse his emperor. "The army, sire, parts of it only look splendid on parade."

The uniforms in the ballroom were quite magnificent. Hussars glittered in their green jackets, their scarlet shakos, all yellow corded, their black and yellow feathers, their red breeches with broken yellow stripe, their green cloaks bordered with black fur, their red saddle clothes with black, white and yellow piping. And of course, there were the grenadiers with their white tunics, the officers with their gold sashes, the Uhlans with their green coats and red waistcoats, the engineers with their pale blue tailcoats, the gunners with their cinnamon tailcoats, the dragoons with their shining breastplates and fire on their helmets, the Jaegers with their light blue tunics ...

The Emperor was intoxicated by the splendour of his own imperial army but he did not want to hear about uniforms, he wanted to know about the fighting capacity and the mobilised strength of his eight hundred thousand men. He did not know that Radetzky and the Adjutant-General, Count Grunne, had between them allowed the army to run-down, and that none of his divisional commanders actually knew anything about war. He did not want to be implicated himself by hearing that Austrian officers liked nothing better than to play at soldiers, and that the vast majority dreaded any call to arms.

"Sire. This is the French we are fighting, not just Piedmont." Gyulai spirits were at the lowest ebb of his entire career. He could not convince the Emperor that their preparation for this war was ill-prepared, the conflict ill-advised, and the army ill-equipped.

"We are fighting on our terrain, Field-Marshall. By the time the French arrive, they should be ill-prepared and ill-equipped." The Emperor slapped the commander on his back "Come, Gyulai, what that old ass Radetzky could get a way with, you surely can!"

The matter was at a close. The supreme Commander-in Chief had given his field marshal his orders. He turned and waved to his wife who was still in earnest conversation with the Countess Rostov.

"Now, Olli, what is the latest about the whereabouts of the travelling Count Rostov?" The Empress had a grin on her face as if she was expecting Olive to tell her something naughty. It did not seem to matter to her now that the fate of Italy hung in the hands of her husband. Politics was the failure of all men. They endeavoured to put the world to rights and only succeeded in putting it to wrong. They filled their heads with notions of principle and ideal, yet when it was all over, they were left disillusioned and shattered.

Why? That was always the question on a woman's mind. Why did men destroy themselves and the happiness of the women about them. Invariably the loved their mothers but treated their wives like children. It was so with Franz Josef. It was so with Grigori.

Olive had not heard from Grigori, and she had said nothing to Marie about his visit to her, but since that night, Olive and Marie had grown closer, and Olive suspected that Marie knew too he was gone for good. Olive totally forgave Marie for everything. The regime in the house had relaxed, and despite Grigori's desire that she moved, she remained at the house in the Singerstrasse, and began to receive guests, including the Empress, who also became friendly with Countess Festetics.

Sisi was only one year older than Olive, and she had advice to offer about everything, some sensible, some crass, some silly, but nevertheless, it was advice she had from no-one else. Olive, in turn, managed to tell Sisi about the world, the real world outside the court, or in the opera house, where people were sometimes happy, sometimes sad, sometimes a little worried about the future. For the Empress, the befriending of the Countess Rostov was a breath of spring into her institutionalised life. Here, thought the Empress, was a Russian, a woman as beautiful as herself, who understood what it was like to be a foreigner in Vienna, someone near her own age who was fun and knew how to laugh and joke and be her age. In Olive, Sisi had found a friend she could confide in, someone who was not trying to make her something she was not, someone who understood what it was like to live a lie, for deep down Sisi did not feel like an empress, she felt like an imposter, someone who pretended to be something she was not, someone who carried shame and deceit around with her every living moment

Olive understood these feelings for obvious reasons. She had never been able to meet the standard required of her by Grigori. She was his Pygmalion, and she had lived in the shadow of Grigori as much as Sisi lived in the shadow of the Emperor. From the moment she had met Grigori, he had been her guide, the decision maker, the master of their relationship, and she had time and time again asked herself the question 'Why me?'

Yet life has strange ways of twisting and turning and coming out ways that none ever expected. To have befriended the Empress of Austria was to have thought of the impossible when she had been a child on the land of Russia. From serf to the Court of Vienna, the leap was beyond the imagination of writers or poets. It was a fiction, yet it was real and it was happening to her. Likewise for the girl from Bavaria, to find herself viewed as beauty incarnate, revered as a goddess by the peasantry, and to live in a string of enchanted castles, was a dream which she could never awaken from. Nothing seemed real, nothing at all except her horses, her dogs, and Olive Vanya. For the Empress had come to rely on Olive Vanya, and demanded more and more of her time, until at length Olive began to feel the same claustrophobic atmosphere of the court, the same stale smell of old age and decay, the same loathing and hatred of the entire imperial system, as Sisi did.

13

Things came to a head one year after the defeats of Magenta and Solfarino and the loss of Italy. The Empress had been imbued enough by Austria and the Emperor. Of the first, she was certain, of the latter she was ambiguous and undecided. She had given the Emperor two girls Sophie and Gisela. In the care of her children she had a war with Arch-Duchess Sophie, to the extent that

Franzi had told his mother outright that he would no longer put up with her attempts to take the two girls entirely away from her. In the end little Sophie had died in Budapest, and Sisi had almost gone out of her mind. Then she gave birth to Rudolf, the heir to the Habsburg throne, and all was bliss. Then, with the war in Italy, Franz Josef had relieved Gyulai as commander-in-chief after losing to the French at Magenta, and gone there to head the army himself.

The Battle of Solfarino was an unmitigated disaster for Austria. It was the end of June and the heat on the north Italian plain was phenomenal. Disease as well as hunger was rife. The French were dying of malaria, and the Austrians had fifty thousand sick men in their lines. Along the battle-lines there was very little shade and practically no water. The local peasant children were dying of thirst, the drought had turned the richest part of the Empire prematurely brown. Drawn against each other - the French and Piedmontese with one hundred and forty thousand men, the Austrians one hundred and thirty thousand - were numbers on a scale that even Napoleon Bonaparte the inventor of mass armies had never managed to control. By the start of the day, two hundred and seventy thousand men, forty thousand horses, seven hundred guns were engaged in a fifteen-mile front. The battle raged all morning and into the afternoon. At half past four the heat broke. The entire battlefield was hit by violent thunder, lightning, hail, flooding, and in a matter of moments, the whole vast battlefield was blotted out. The battle was over. Forty thousand men lay dead and dying in the terrible heat of the battlefield for two days, dying of exposure, hunger, gangrene and sheer exhaustion. Peasants returning to their ruined farms were conscripted to bury the dead and burn the horses. It took eight days.

Franz Josef had written to Sisi saying 'I do not feel that I am to blame'. He had lost Lombardy, and were it not for the intervention of Prussia, and an armistice with Napoleon III, Venetia would have been lost too.

*

Sisi had not been overwhelmed by her duties as an Empress but after the disgrace of Solferino, she was disgusted by the pretence and ritual of behaving as if nothing had happened. Franzi would not speak to her on the matter, so she quite literally, refused to have any more to do with imperial pomp. She shut herself away, so that even for long stretches, Olive Vanya did not see her. Then, one day, quite out of the blue, she called on Olive backstage at the Opera. There was much commotion and curtseying and 'your highness' before Empress Elizabeth gained access to Olive in make-up for rehearsal of Balfe's The Bohemian Girl, in which, Olive sung the part of Arline.

"My dear, Olli" broke down the Empress, embarrassing Olive before settling uncomfortably on a chair littered with the accoutrements of the opera profession. "I

have come to ask if you will come with me."
"Come where, Sisi?" Olive asked in the
tome of familiarity that Sisi had always
enjoyed. She had been running through her
scales, and was now finding it difficult to
concentrate on what Sisi was saying to her.
"Madeira."
"Where is that, Sisi?" She had never been
strong on geography "Is it a state visit to
Bohemia or something you want me to
come on?" Olive laughed. Quite by chance
she had made a joke that connected a part
of the empire with the opera she was in,
but she suddenly realised that the Sisi she
had first met riding at Laxenburg almost
two years before was not the same Sisi as
now.
"Madeira is in the Canary Islands in the
middle of the Atlantic, Olli" the Empress
replied in a dull tone "I'm leaving Franzi."
The first thing that came into Olive's mind
was to say the conventional thing 'No, you
are making a terrible mistake. You can't
leave our husband, think of the scandal.'
But Olive loved Sisi, and wanted the best
for her, not what the world wanted best for
Franz Josef. She knew Sisi had made up
her mind. The man had made her ill, not by
mental cruelty or harshness, but by
neglect. Here, was the most beautiful
woman in all of Europe, the world said so,
lonely, bitter, and going out of her mind
because of lack of love, lack of company,
lack of warmth, lack of humanity. The Court
of Vienna, with its imperial, callous nature
had sucked the life out of Sisi and left her
anorexic, mentally unstable, unable to bring

her children up as she wished, and married to a husband who never talked to her about anything more serious than the troubles of the Empire.

"Franz Josef is a martyr for Austria, Sisi" Olive responded "while you have been a martyr for Franz Josef. I understand how you feel. Yes, I will come to Madeira."

"Oh Olli!" she said clapping her hands together. ""But what about the Count?" she asked hesitantly.

"He's dead. I had an official letter about three months ago from the Ministry of War saying that he had died at Solferino."

"What was he doing there, Olli." the Empress asked softly, not knowing how to take the news. The friend had always been secretive about the Count, but not to tell her that he was dead surprised her, for Olive was one of her closest friends.

"They said that he had been working at the Milan Opera House when the Piedmontese had occupied the city, and joined the refugees heading east into Venetia. Just before the battle of Solferino, he was mistaken for a French spy, and shot. The Ministry of War said, as his widow, they regretted the error, but as he was a foreign citizen, I am not entitled to compensation."

"What? Leave this matter with me, Olli. I'll take it up with Franz Josef."

"No, Sisi, let the matter rest. That's why I didn't mention it before now. It is how Grigori would want it to be." She had forgiven him. For a while after Grigori had gone she had hated him, despised him for the deceit, the four years of living as his wife, waiting for him, living for him, waiting for him to make love to her, which he had not done until their last parting. Now he was dead, the pain had gone, and she began to remember only the good times, the happy times, the triumphs.

"If you wish, Olive Vanya, but I don't understand." She had never been at all clear about Olive's relationship with the fabled Count Rostov who she had never met. "What about your singing?" the Empress asked, more out of reassurance than doubt about Olive's future.

"I've sung before a Habsburg Emperor, dear Sisi, so I should have no problem finding work elsewhere if I ever return to it." Olive knew she was sacrificing her career for Sisi, but there are moments in life when one's own ambitions are worth nothing when measured against another person's despair.

"It will only be for a little while until I recover my health" the Empress confessed to her friend. However, in the matter of relationships, both Sisi and Olive were young and inexperienced. Neither of them knew what was ahead of them. The Empress Elizabeth was twenty-two, and as we know, Olive Vanya was just one year younger, and at that age, no woman or man can predict in matters of health or human relationships, the outcome of the rest of her, or his life.

14

They had arrived in late November '60

aboard the *Victoria and Albert* yacht. It would have been easier had they sailed from Venice, but Franz Josef did not have a suitable vessel for his wife's *sickness leave*, as it was called, and instead it was arranged that she should sail from Antwerp aboard the yacht of the English royal family. Of course, most of the big families of Europe were shocked that Elizabeth had found it necessary to be *ill* at a time when things had been going terribly wrong for Franz Josef and the Empire. However, Sisi was her own woman, and companioned by Olive Vanya and a number of ladies in waiting, they descended down the gangway on Funchal, the main town of Madeira, and caused an immediate stir. The entire quay was thronged with children waving little red and white Austrian cloth flags; mothers wanting their babies kissed; men standing with their caps in their hands; and even little old ladies giving their blessings and weeping at the beautiful dress and radiant face of the Empress.

Sisi detested it, it was everything she had hoped to escape from, the attention, the constant glare of the public, but she put on a good smile, waved, and the crowd cheered. After the polite introductions to the Portuguese Governor of the islands, the local dignitaries and their wives, in private Sisi gave unmistakable signals to the Governor that she had come to Madeira to rest, and not as many might have hope for, extravagant balls or dinner parties.

Not that this was very likely. All Olive Vanya could see was that the Madeira's were a collection of small islands almost six hundred kilometres west of the Moroccan coast of Africa, and that they appeared to be an important stopping off place for merchant ships plying the trading routes down the African coast and round the Horn to India. On the tour of the town given by the Governor, she saw rubber on a trader-ship from Para at the mouth of the Amazon basin, and sugar being loaded on to a ship from Lisbon. A third ship was taking on fish for a journey across the Atlantic to the Demerara. The Governor explained - in excellent French - that many stopped to take on sugar, wine, bananas, or fish - it was these things that were the economic life-blood of the islands that sustained a dense population of plantation owners, labourers, fishermen and peasants and their immediate families. The peasants, the Governor said, by far outnumbered all the rest, and of Portuguese origin, they had brought with them the characteristics of rural Portugal.

The islands themselves were part of a group of volcanic origin, many which were very old and had been worn down by erosion. It had been many years since the last eruption, but it was a constant concern that made farming on the mountainsides very difficult. The Governor added that it was unfortunate that the Empress had chosen the winter months to come to Madeira as it rained a lot.

"Sir," Sisi replied in French that hinted at her Bavarian accent "if you had to spend winter in Austria, you would know that a little rain is the least of my problems. Today, touching land and seeing the sun shine on your little town after four days at sea, was one of the most wonderful moments of my life!"

The Governor thought that the Empress was just being witty and polite, but Olive knew that Sisi honestly meant every word, for she could see that even in the few hours they had been on the island, a transformation had occurred which had lifted Sisi out of her depression. But it did not last long, for as soon as they had settled into the large plantation house that was to be their new home for the length of their stay, Sisi broke down into a fit of sobbing, and shut herself away in her large bedroom which overlooked the sea.

However hard she tried, Olive could not penetrate the veil of depression that had led Sisi to cut herself off from the rest of the world. Some mornings she would be bright and cheerful and they would go for long rides up the mountain tracks in search of some rare flower or plant she had read about in a book; other mornings she would stay in bed to well past eleven, refusing to be served breakfast, writing long letters of woe to Franz Josef. On those occasions she did not look like an Empress, but like a tired mother of three, unloved by her husband, denied access to her children by her mother-in-law, who with nothing to live for, lived every moment in pain.

Yet, as the months went by, Sisi began to be more settled in her behaviour. She began to speak less and less about herself and more about the things of the world; the shape of her fingernails, the curl of her hair, the colour in her cheeks. Life had returned to her, and she began to crave company, seek excitement, and to arrange selective little parties for her small entourage of Olive Vanya, two ladies-in-waiting, her physician, her nurse, and five servants.

So after five months of boredom on Madeira, the Empress of Austria threw her first public party and invited the Governor and anyone who was anyone to come. She did not care if the peasants showed up - she was ready for the world!

The night of the party Sisi was radiant, to the extent that for the first time, Olive thought of herself as ugly. She had not enjoyed her time with Sisi; it had been difficult and fraught with anxious moments because the Empress had tried to do away with herself a couple of times. On one occasion she had caught Sisi attempting to slit her own wrists, and a slap on Sisi's face had been the only way to get her to drop the broken piece of mirror in her hand. Besides her lay a letter from Franz Josef saying that he had lost Lombardy for good, and that he was having difficulties with the Prussians etc etc. There was no mention of the children, only a short end pleading from him for her to come home to Austria, that he missed her. To Olive it had been like a letter that a father would send a daughter, not an Emperor to his beloved wife.

There had been other draining moments, to the extent, that Olive herself felt drained. It was therefore with some relief that she looked forward to the party; an opportunity to enjoy herself, for it was a gloomy house despite its spacious interior and large outside balconies.

In all there were about eighty guests and the floorboards of the house creaked under the weight of evening gowns and pearls. It was not the splendour of the Vienna Court, for despite their large houses, the wealthy of Madeira were plantation owners, not aristocrats, and in this respect, their educations in Lisbon and Madrid, had not prepared them for audiences with royalty. However, they were fine gentlemen and ladies, and as the custom of the Vienna Court had been one of Spanish etiquette, the bridging of mores between Austria and Portugal met mutually with a flicking of fans and clicking of heels, as Sisi, Olive, the ladies-in-waiting, the physician, and the Nurse, were introduced in turn to the new arrivals.

By Court standards it was a very informal affair, and the Empress moved about freely speaking to her guests, trying out her newly-learned Portuguese, falling back when necessary into French, and on one occasion, conversing in Danish with a plantation owner's wife from Copenhagen.

Olive was less adept at Portuguese and her French lacked the vocabulary to talk in depth about shipping or sugar crops. She did however fall into conversation with a young American who spoke German. She discovered he was on his way to Venice to be the new American consul.

"But you are so young? How did you get such a post? In Austria nearly everyone in political service was a bald and paunched."

"Why" said the young twenty-four year old American from Ohio "I wrote the campaign biography for Mr. Lincoln. He was elected in November, sworn in in January, and here I am in April, on my way to serve the President in Europe." His face beamed with innocence and good manners.

Olive knew nothing about Americans. "Are you saying that you were made a Consul because you wrote just one thing?" She found it hard to believe. In Austria, the greatest Austrian poet of the day, Franz Grillparzer, her German tutor, was looked upon as little better than a peasant by the Austrian courtiers.

"Not just anything, Countess, I wrote the life story of the greatest man in American presidential history." He was a devoted new republican.

"So George Washington was not so good?" asked Olive in a tone that made it sound as though the American had said it first.

"George Washington is the greatest man in American history, but he was not the greatest president." Howells found himself being drawn in by Olive. Their eyes met. She looked down at his feet. It was something that Sisi had taught her. 'When confronted by a young attractive man who might want to seduce you, look at his feet. If he is insecure of his dress sense he will ask you what is wrong with his shoes. If he is unsure of his own looks, he will ask you if there is anything wrong with you. If he is a brute he will force you to look at him. If however he knows that you are playing with him, he will make some other conversation, or wait patiently until you look up again, then speak.'

What Howells did next made Olive laugh; she nearly spilt the glass of champagne in her hand.

"Countess" he said pleadingly "let's not have the greatest men in America come between us." He lifted her chin with his forefinger. "Look at me, I have nothing to be ashamed of. My shoes are polished, my looks at fine, and I can stand as straight as any man." He stepped forward "Now, Countess, will you do me the pleasure of a walk in the Madeira air, for as yet I have had none, and I sail in two days."

William Dean Howells was an aspiring poet of mediocre talents whose father was a poor, idealistic Mid-West journalist, who had introduced his son to the same profession. He took her by the arm and she did not protest. However they were not long in the sweet spring air filled with bougainvillea and frangipani when Howells, talking about the stars and the moon, grabbed her and kissed her. She did not struggle, but at the end of the kiss, she slapped him across the face with her fan.

"Excuse me!" he howled in a voice that went all the way back to his childhood in his little Ohio town near the Great Lakes.

"You forgot to ask me, Mr. Howells." She opened her fan and began to stir the air. "It is not acceptable where I come from ..." She was going to explain further, but she changed her mind.

"Where do you come from, Countess?" he replied having recovered his composure. He had come to the conclusion that Olive was not Austrian but something strange and exotic and totally unexpected.

Olive ignored his question, she was not going to drag her past up and present it to this impolite American. "Where I come from, gentlemen don't kiss other men's wives without first finding out where the husband is."

Howells laughed, "You Europeans sure are funny. It's the talk of the town that you women folk have been living up here all on your own for months without seeing anybody. But I saw you in town yesterday, Countess, buying little things to make yourself nice for tonight." This surprised Olive, but when she thought about it, it did not seem so unbelievable, for everywhere she and the others went in Funchal, small crowds would gather to gaze at them. "The moment I saw you, I say's to myself, Will, there is the most beautiful women you have ever seen in your whole life. So I asked some questions, found out that the Count Rostov was dead nigh on two years. I says, Will, what's a beautiful gal like that going around with a face like a long steer in a Chicago freight-wagon. It's not right. So I put off my sailing until the day after tomorrow, paid some guy ten dollars for my outfit, and came along to the shindig to see if I could make a gal smile." It was not Howells normal way of speaking; it was put on for effect.

Olive blushed. She had never been spoken to this way before, and despite its strangeness, and the language, she liked it for its honesty. However, the American's kiss had not stirred anything in her, and she felt no need to repeat the experience.

At her insistence, they returned to the party. Sisi was at the piano playing a Viennese waltz, surrounded by many of her guests

"Olli!" she cried on seeing her friend "Come sing for us." Sisi was in a gay mood. She'd had a few glasses of champagne and was beaming with vitality.

To the delight of everyone in the room, Olive sang from Bizet's Carmen, and by a simple arrangement of furniture, re-enacted the scene of Carmen's seduction of the young soldier, using a bewildered and embarrassed Mr. Howells as the young soldier mesmerised by the temptress.

*

Olive was surprised the morning after the party when William Howells came to the plantation house to apologise to the Countess for his ungentlemanly behaviour in the garden the previous evening. He had drank too much, and fully deserved the humiliation he had suffered during the performance.

"Apology accept, Herr Howells" she said kindly, for she could see that he was not a man who made a habit of asking for forgiveness. He was a curious man; polite, but not a flatterer; refined, but not stuffy. He had suffered enormously the evening before. At first the prey of his desires under the stars, Olive had become under the party lights, the predator, the one teasing with him, playing with him. She had wrapped herself round him in front of eighty people in dinner dress and terrified him with her trained operatic voice. At one stage she had actually run her hands down the entire length of his body. But, he had not, like many other men might have done, rushed from the room in shame, but bravely borne the ordeal until she had finished her song, and then managed to slip away when the guests had surrounded her demanding she sang another song.

Olive had not meant to humiliate him, only to teach him a lesson; that what looks beautiful on the outside might not be so beautiful on the inside. "Would you like some tea." she asked him. "The clippers from India frequently stop here."

"No thanks, mam. I have found a ship sailing for Naples today, and cannot wait until tomorrow after all. The Rebs have bombarded Fort Sumter and I need to get to Europe at all speed to take the Union's cause. It don't look good me hanging around with my country at war with itself." A look of regret crossed his face.

Olive was not fully aware of the pressing nature of the young man's problems, but she had seen before in Austria the same urgency with which men threw themselves into diplomacy and politics before all else.

"So, Countess, please excuse my hurry, the captain's waiting for me to board, and if I hold him up any more, he'll sail without me."

Olive offered her hand and Howell's put ever so gently to his lips. Here, thought Olive, was a gentleman after all, a slightly wild and impulsive one, but nevertheless, a gentleman. She was now ready to fully forgive him for the kiss. He had earned it.

"Viel Gluck, Mister Howells, perhaps we will meet again."

"Auf weidersein, Countess Rostov." He did not click his heels as an Austrian might, but instead gave a little salute with his right hand to the side of his forehead. He took two steps back and turned. One of the servants handed him his hat. As a final gesture he bowed and said "Madam, American women are the finest in the world, but as yet I have still to meet one who compares with you." He smiled in a modest way and added "If it were not for the war, I'd impel you to visit her" meaning America "for I have friends in New England who could paint a likeness of you that would make you famous across the land."

"Then it is well "Olive replied in an instant "that we have the art of the photograph now to save your friends the pain of the task."

At this final remark made by Olive he laughed, bowed again, and left by carriage at some speed towards the harbour, to catch his passage, and to take up to his new post as Lincoln's American Consul in Venice.

*

One month later the Empress declared that

she was well enough to go home to Austria. Everyone was relieved, for life in Madeira was slow, and for an entourage whose average age was a mere twenty-three, an island in the Atlantic was an exile on par with Emperor Napoleon's banishment to St. Helena.

Everyone was in good spirits, none more so than Sisi who was excited at the prospect of seeing her children after an absence of six months. She confided to Olive that she had missed her horses more than Franz Josef, but it was meant as a joke, and Olive took it as one, though deep down she felt that there was some truth in the statement.

They departed on the *Victoria and Albert* that had arrived some days before from Gibraltar with Queen Victoria's son, Prince Edward, Prince of Wales, a young man of eighteen. The farewell from Madeira was one of tears and joy, for almost the entire population of the main island came to wave at the Empress of Austria and the future King of England. The harbour was crowded with a flotilla of small boats surrounding the royal yacht; the quay was awash with the little Austrian flags of the year before, and some newer looking little British flags which had been distributed by the British Consul for the occasion. There was such a heave and surge on the quay when the Empress arrived in her carriage, that one man fell into the waters of the harbour and had to be rescued by one of the flotilla boats. When they finally hauled him into the boat and he waved merrily at the crowd, a great roar went up that drowned out the

Governor's parting speech from the quay. The Empress was presented with a gift of an engraved pair of silver wine goblets and a one hundred year old bottle of port, and a duly inscribed parchment declaring the people of Madeira's fondest greetings to her husband, the Emperor Franz Josef.

At one point Olive thought it was all going to be too much for Sisi and she would break down into tears, but no, this was a new Sisi, a much tougher Empress of Austria than the one she had arrived with six months before, and she was proud of her. Of her own feelings, Olive was a little sad to be leaving Madeira, she had enjoyed the pleasant climate and the intimate companionship of the ladies in waiting and the staff, even the one who Olive knew had been passing secret information about the Empress's condition to Franz Josef in Vienna. They had all pulled together to get Sisi well, and in this they had succeeded through dark days and troubled nights to bring about. They were proud of their achievement, as was the Governor of Madeira who had been the only one outside their small circle who had realised how seriously disturbed Sisi had been. He had done everything he possibly could to make her stay easier, and for this, the Empress thanked him on behalf of the Emperor of Austria and conferred on him an Order of the Empire.

The Prince of Wales was taken aback by the popularity of the Empress, and by her beauty. The first three days of the sail to Trieste he had only eyes for her, but for the last three days his eyes had switched to feasting on Olive Vanya. It was an embarrassing situation, for the Prince was very charming; whereas the Empress was married and had no idea that the Prince was trying to seduce her, Olive Vanya on the other hand, without the frightening figure of Franz Josef and the honour of the whole Austrian Empire to protect her, had to resort to more cunning ways to keep the amorous Prince out of her cabin.

At first, her flight from the Prince was a delightful game of hide and seek, the odd stolen glance, the chance encounter alone on deck; but it soon became something rather more threatening - a pinching of her bottom, suggestive remarks, a knocking on her door after midnight, and on the last night at sea, in one unguarded moment when she had forgotten to lock her cabin door, the discovery of the Prince naked beside her, pressing his manhood on her.

In shock she kicked him, knocked him from her berth, on to the floor. He yelled.

"Why did you do that, you little minx?" The future King of England lay sprawled on a Persian rug whinnying like a schoolboy.

Olive could not answer. She had been crept up on in the dark when she was a child so many times by Tapiq that she had promised herself that she would never allow it to happen again.

"Have you ever had a woman, you arrogant little boy?" she said sternly to him like some wise nanny scolding her miserable spoilt charge.

"Of course I have ..." He was lying.

"What's it like then?"

"I don't know .... " he hesitated, trying to make something up "It's like .... "

"I'll tell you what it's like " Olive interrupted him "It's like champagne. Once you've had a sip of it, you want more and more, and you can never get enough."

"Is it?" The Prince uttered rather stupidly.

"You're a sad case" Olive laughed. She could not help but laugh at this silly little boy with all the breeding that money and position could buy, who had to pretend that he was not a virgin. "Come here."

He went to her. She laid him on his back and she showed him what it was like to enter a woman for the first time. He squealed a little and held on to the bar at the end of the berth, but she slapped him on the chest.

"Don't squeal! Only pigs squeal." It did not take her long to educate him.

*

Dawn broke over the Adriatic coast, and there were stirrings on deck as they prepared to change the watch. Olive kicked the Prince awake. He was so startled; he bumped his head on a bulkhead.

"Owwl! That hurt."

"Go on, Eddie, get back to your own cabin before I kick you again."

He stumbled out of the bunk and gathered up his clothes, which were strewn, on the floor. "Where did you learn to do those things?"

"What things?" She was tired of him. He asked too many questions. She wanted him out of her cabin before Sisi in the cabin next door woke up.

"Those things you showed me last night." The Prince tried to kiss her.

"You lost your virginity to a widow, Eddie." She pushed him away. "Last night you got the best champagne of your life. From now on it'll be sip after sip, and you'll never be satisfied. When we see each other again, pretend it didn't happen."

Olive opened her cabin door and pushed him out. He began to protest, but Olive laughed and threw the bucket of water that was outside her door all over him. He squealed.

"Piggy" she shouted after him.

"Rotter!" he called back.

She laughed again. He was just a young boy. He was no Grigori Rostov. Even two years after his death, and three years since she had seen him, she was still in love with Grigori. She knew that no man could ever replace him; he had taken her from being a peasant girl and turned her into a Countess, with an Empress as a friend, and little boy Princes to play with. Yet, after seven years of such experiences, she had come to realise that she had become imprisoned like Sisi and Edward. Her existence had no meaning. She was a doll, a plaything for them, for others. She did not understand herself, and perhaps that is why she reacted with such force when she was unexpectedly set-upon by men who were overwhelmed by her beauty. She would have liked to react differently, but she did not want to look deeper and delve into her years in Constantinople; she buried the experience in a past she could tell no one about. Inside herself she felt dirty and soiled, as if all the beauty of the outside was matched by an equivalent evil inside. Others like Eddie, she thought, saw only the surface, the beauty of her body, not the ugliness of her mind.

It was for this reason that Olive understood the Empress, for inside both felt the same hatred for the world and what it had done to them. Eddie had been drawn to her for a different reason, because he was a dumb, stupid boy, who had received no love from his mother, and so without knowing it hated of all women, and treated them all as objects.

Olive felt much the same about men. No one had ever attempted to get inside her to find the real Olive Vanya, not even Grigori. He had made her into something that was his own creation, he never once had tried to find out whom she really was, and as a result, she had begun to feel like Mary Shelley's Frankenstein creation, a creature with a body, but with the wrong brain. She fully understood why Sisi had tried to slit her own wrists, for like Olive, Sisi had the body of an Empress, but as Franz Josef's creation, he had chosen the wrong brain and failed to recognise that fact.

The truth of the matter was that while Frankenstein was a piece of fiction created by an author, Sisi, unlike Olive, was a real human being who had refused to be re-created. So too was Eddie, the future king of England, and Mr. Howells, the most human of men, who created as Lincoln's man, had created Lincoln himself by writing his biography, to the extent that they had created each other.

Olive felt that the time had come to undo Grigori's work. No matter what, there had to be more to life than royalty and riches and the small circle of 'created' people Olive moved amongst. There had to be a whole wide world out there waiting to to be explored, a land where people, rather than being made by others, made themselves. If there was such a land she would find it, for anything had to be better than the bizarre world she had come to inhabit.

15

One month after the return to Vienna, Sisi was a complete wreck again. Between them, Franz Josef and his evil mother Grand-Duchess Sophie, had reduced her to tears, refusing her an active part in the education of her children.

Sisi broke off from the Habsburgs and left for Corfu. Olive Vanya went as far as Venice with her, hugged and kissed her goodbye, on board the fleet vessel taking her the half-day's sail southwards. She had begged Olive to go with her, but Olive had made her own arrangements, so falling upon the person nearest at hand, Sisi had invited Marie Festetics to take Olive's place as her companion, and Marie had accepted.

Olive was heavy-hearted as she saw Sisi wave to her for the last time. She knew they would never meet again, and she sensed that Sisi knew this too. Marie had made light of the parting saying that they would all be together in Vienna again within three months, but Marie had only been trying to smooth over the cracks of a crumbling facade. All of their lives were a mess, and they knew it. Even Marie, for the sake of Olive and her own reputation, had to hide the fact that she had been the mistress of Count Rostov. Any breath of scandal and Franz Joseph would have prevented Sisi from having contact with either of them, for quite unseen to the public eye, Franz Josef controlled the finances, the houses, the travel arrangements, and the movements of his wife. It had been his suggestion that if she could not stand Vienna, then she go to Corfu, a Greek speaking island in Dalmatia, the most southerly province of the Empire.

Olive could not face living in Austria any more. After the Empress's ship had gone beyond reasonable sight, she had taken a carriage to the American Consul's house.

"Countess Rostov!" William Howells gaped with surprise when she was shown into his shabby little office. He was dressed in black and had been looking out the window watching a Venetian girl. She was seated on a bench that was fixed between two elms and was surrounded by a group of little street urchins. For a moment she had leaned her head against one of the elms as if faint with the attention. She had a bodice and petticoat of different colours, and a handkerchief tied neatly about her head with the point behind. On her hands were gloves without fingers, and she wore about her neck, a guitar. The children thought she looked very pretty, but to Howells, she looked very ill. They were urging her to play.

"Oh che bei ragazzi! Che visi lieti!" Oh, what fine boys, what happy faces she said to them, and began to play. She tried to sing, but her voice seemed to fail her, and she shook her head smilingly "Stanca! Stanca!", meaning that she was too weary.

"Rosaura! Rosaura!" they chanted as if they had known her all their lives, trying to make her sing, but suddenly, something had diverted the attention of the urchins and they had all run off and deserted the girl under the elm trees. Rosaura seemed relieved, curled her legs up on to the bench and sunk her chin into her knees and closed her eyes. It was at this point that Olive was shown into his presence. He ushered her into a chair.

"I want to go to America, Mr. Howells." Olive was dressed in a black outfit that made her look very serious until she smiled.

"America? Why?" He seemed shocked. He did not like her in black; it made her look too solemn, and did not seem right on someone so young.

"You are the American Consul, are you not?"

"Yes." The strangeness of her request had begun to seem quite normal.

"Where do you suggest I travel too? Ohio?" Olive did not have any idea about geography. She knew that America was on the other side of the Atlantic; she had heard of Washington because of George Washington; and she had heard of Ohio from Mr. Howells himself.

"Well ... " He remembered what he had said to her in Madeira "Ohio's not the prettiest state in America. I suggest you start with Rhode Island. Its about half way between New York and Boston. I have friends in Newport who you would get on famously with."

"Is there an Opera House there?" Olive had to think about making a living, whatever savings she had had left over from her singing was gone, and the monies raised from the sale of her possessions in Vienna was not substantial. Sisi had never concerned herself about money or understood the need for it, Franz Josef paid for everything, and therefore had not even asked Olive what she was going to live on when she got to America. Marie, more understanding of the ways of the world, had provided a sum that Grigori had left in trust for her that would enable her to exist moderately for a year at the level of a ballerina or an opera singer, but not in the opulence she had become accustomed to in Vienna.

"No. But New York and Boston. My friends will guide you, have no fear." He stopped, for he could suddenly hear the sound of a guitar. He looked out the window again. Rosaura, once more surrounded by the urchins, was playing.

"Are you familiar with Ralph Waldo Emerson, Countess?" he asked her. She shook her head. "Deep in the man sits fast his fate, to mound his fortunes mean or great." Olive could not understand what he had said, for Howells had resorted to his native American language. "It was Emerson who made me interested in Europe" he said returning to German. He took Olive by the hand and led her to the window. He pointed to the girl on the bench below.

"The Sun goes down, and with him takes the coarseness of my poor attire; the fair moon mounts, and aye the flame of Gypsy beauty blazes higher." He was pleased with is own powers of memory. "There, below, Countess" William Howells added "is the Europe I read in Emerson as a boy. A guitar playing gypsy girl. Have you ever seen anything more European than that? She'd make a fortune in America."

Olive looked down on the poor pale-face girl and instantly recognised the suffering she must have undergone to have become the embodiment of the American's Europe. She watched as Howells continued to stare at the girl in fascination, but she turned from the window, for the girl on the Venice bench was another Cinderella waiting for a Prince Charming.

"What would you say if I said I wanted to take that girl to America with me?" Olive was not serious; she was only testing him out.

"What a wonderful idea! Would she go with you?" Howells was enthusiastic.

"I don't think she would survive the journey, do you. And besides, I think she

would be happier here." Olive did not want
to create her own creatures.

"How could she be happy with being poor
and shoeless?"

"We cannot go around changing the world
to fulfil our own fantasies. That is why we
have poets. They fulfil our fantasies on
paper. Real life is much more complex than
mere wealth and happiness."

Howells turned from the window. "I do not
like to hear negative talk, Countess, it hurts
my feelings, for I believe in Jefferson's
Declaration that all men are created equal,
women too. That is why I am opposed to
the Confederacy and slavery, the conditions
that bring men into the world unequal. For
a man to be owned by another man, like a
farmer owned a cow, or a rider a horse,
upsets my whole being. It is this more than
anything that makes me a Lincoln man -
the abolition of slavery." He looked out the
window again. "You are lucky, madam, to
have been born without poverty. I cannot
confess the same luxury and must work for
my daily bread, but that girl out there, she
must beg for hers."

"That is her work, Mr. Howells, and she is
well trained to it. She will not thank you for
any intervention. To take a young girl to
another country, she has probably not even
heard of, is a cruel thing to do. Believe me,
I know."

"How do you know, Countess?" Howells was
angry. "It would appear to me that poverty
would be something you passed in the
streets but knew nothing about." After the
words had tumbled from his mouth, he

suddenly felt that he had gone too far and that the Countess would slap him again or bid him good day. She frightened him because he could not guess how she would react.

"You are very wrong, Mr. Howells. I will not go into detail, but I can tell you that there is little difference between a gypsy girl and an Empress. A gypsy girl is unmistakably plain and ordinary; an Empress mistakenly beautiful and complicated. It is all a matter of perception, for gypsy and empress are both women born equal, but elevated by society to be unequal. This is the dilemma of all societies. They may create the conditions to be born equal, but they cannot control the circumstances that produce inequality. Certainly, I am also for the abolition of slavery, I think that Russia needs a Lincoln, Austria needs a Lincoln, but at what cost? Civil War is not a political solution - it is a last resort when words fail, ideals conflict. Equal vigour plus equal resistance equates to chaos."

"I respect your views, Countess" He had met an intellectual equal and it surprised him. In fact everything about her surprised him. She was unreal. He asked himself the same stupid question that men throughout time had asked about beautiful women - how could anyone so beautiful be so intelligent? He just did not know; he felt out of his league, and thought it just as well he had his Vermont-born sweetheart coming out in the Fall to visit him. "Now, as for the matter in hand. I'll arrange papers for you. But it will have to be tomorrow ... I have to attend the funeral of the British consul today."

"He was an associate of my late husband." Olive replied with dignity. She was dressed in black to attend the funeral herself. Grigori had regularly visited Venice before his death, and the Consul had stayed at Marie Fenestics house in Vienna.

"It's a small world, ain't it", Howells exclaimed "George James was British Consul at Richmond, Virginia, back in fifty-two. He was a writer of novels, and my father interviewed him for his paper. He took me along to meet him." Howells went pensive, then chuckled "My father wrote that his books lacked invention in incident and character, and that although he looked forward to every new James book, he only half knew what he was going to do with his lady and his gentleman. But, Mr. James himself charmed my father, as I was, and I was looking forward to meeting him again after all these years. Then, when I got to Venice, I found out that he had some contagious disease, and I put off visiting him until he was better. Unfortunately he died ... he was only fifty-eight."

Olive thought that a long time to live, but by the looks of William Howells when he said it, he thought it young.

Howells shuffled some papers on his desk and said that the funeral service was to be held in the English church near St. Marks. "Have you ever seen a Venetian funeral procession? Everyone goes by gondola." This seemed to amuse Howells "It'll certainly give me something to write about." The boy from Martin's Ferry, Ohio, had received a good education, but it had been self-taught through books.

He took Olive's arm and escorted her out of his squalid office. They descended to street level and out into the narrow alley running between the office and the canal. The gondolier, who had brought Olive to the office, was still waiting. He chased away the urchins, and then helped her, and William Howells into his craft. As he pushed off, they looked up and saw the girl with the guitar.

"Signori ..... Signore" she pleaded, following along the canal bank with outstretched hand, followed by the band of urchins, looking first at Howells, then Olive. Howells dipped into his pocket and threw her a large coin. "Grazie! Grazie!" she shouted in thanks, putting the palms of her hands together, and bowing. The urchins clamoured around her, pleading with her "Rosaura, Rosaura."

The gondola moved swift away from her. Howells looked at Olive, and she returned the look. He said nothing, but she could see by the quick way he glanced back at the girl and then to her again, that the romantic notion of Europe that he once had, was slowly being replaced by a new confused reality.

16

The voyage to America was a long one. Olive had not appreciated how far away it was, and had she known, she might have thought to reduce the sea journey by travelling by train to France and across the Channel to England where she might have caught a ship to the Americas from Liverpool or Glasgow.

As it was, America was at war with itself. The naval blockade of the southern ports had affected trade and reduced the number of ships plying across the Atlantic. Most countries had declared their neutrality, refusing to take sides in a war that did not concern them directly.

Howells had warned Olive of the difficulties and possible dangers of the journey, but he did not try to dissuade her from setting out. He admired her courage and re-assured her that the fighting would never reach the Northern states, that the rebels were too weak, and that the war would be over in a matter of months. He gave her a number of introductory letters, and had gone as far as to write in advance to his friends in Boston and Newport, that a real Austrian Countess, and an opera singer at that would be calling on them in a matter of weeks, rather than months.

Olive thanked Howells, whom she now called William, for arranging her papers and passage, but he said that he was only too happy to help, and that as Consul, that was part of his job. They parted as friends, not as lovers as either of them might have hoped; he was a highly moral man, a protestant puritan, but not in the old fashioned sense, for he approved of divorce if human happiness was in the balance. However, their discussion in his office had proved to Olive that they were very different culturally, and true enough, when they spent too much time together, it inevitably led to argument and recrimination.

Olive wondered what sort of friends William had in Newport, whether they would be as gentle, well bred and civilised; she could not imagine a society that did not have royalty or nobility. The lack of class structure made it difficult to know if Mr. William Morris Hunt or Mr. Henry James (no relation to the late British consul George James) were any different from any other Mister in America. At least in Europe, a Count was a Count, though as Olive herself knew, a Countess could be an imposter.

In these matters she had to rely totally on William Howells to guide her. The letters she possessed were all to Misters, except for the last, which he had handed her separately as she boarded her ship the *Adriatic*. It was addressed Mr. Lincoln, President.

Why she was given an introduction to the President of the United States mystified Olive. William thought it was obvious.

"You are a friend of the Empress, Olive. That makes you an important person. Mr. Lincoln would be delighted to hear about the Empress Elizabeth. He has seen photographs of her, and considers her the most beautiful woman in the world. Mrs. Lincoln by contrast is very plain."

Olive laughed. Americans were taken in by position and wealth after all, they just did not want to admit it. She kissed the Consul on the cheek.

"Countess, I must object" he said jocularly "What would the President say. I'm only doing my duty." It was a marked difference from the situation under the stars in Madeira.

"Thank you, William."

In the end, Olive had come to like the young American very much. He was kind and thoughtful, and she had enjoyed his company during her time in Venice, which had amounted to just over three weeks, during which time she had taken English lessons.

"Arrivedechi, Countess."

"Goodbye, Mr. Howells" she replied in English. She would miss him very much, but she had learned to part from people without shedding a tear, or letting emotion well-up in her, or to dwell on sadness. "I will tell America how wonderful their man in Venice is."

The ship sailed to schedule, though this time, it was Olive at the stern waving goodbye to someone left standing on the quay waving back.

*

It must have seemed to the old families of America who had arrived with the Plymouth Brethren that the open-door policy of immigration, and the proclamation that it was the Land of the Free, had opened a floodgate that threatened to swamp them. There were in New England strong Republican advocates of a tighter system of immigration control and longer residency before the acquisition of citizenship, but they were shouted down by Democrats as racists and bigots; the Democrats being the party of the immigrants, particularly the Irish.

With the outbreak of the rebellion, all that was put aside, for their was a sudden need on both North and South sides for volunteers. Within months of enlisting, a man was guaranteed citizenship of the United States, though there was some confusion as to whether a conscript in the Confederacy, in the event of defeat of the secessionists, would be considered a citizen or a traitor. However, most men joined conscious of the issues involved - fighting for the industrial slave-free North to save the Union; or fighting on behalf of the agricultural slave-owning South for the right of individual states to leave the Union - it was this split-conscience, that turned a rebellion into a civil war.

At the centre of it all was Abe Lincoln. Popular though he may have been in the North, he had hardly polled a single popular vote in the South because of his anti-slavery program. In defiance, seven, then four more Southern States took Jefferson Davis as their President. Yet, the source of the whole dilemma seemed to be in Thomas Jefferson's Declaration of Independence document itself. The North held rightly so - that all men were created equal, they were endowed by their creator with certain unalienable rights - life, liberty and the pursuit of happiness. The South also contended rightly that governments were instituted among men, deriving their just powers from the consent of the governed; that whenever any form becomes destructive of these ends, it is the right of the people to alter or abolish it, and to institute a new government, laying its foundation on such principles and organizing its powers in such form as to them shall seem most likely to effect their safety and happiness.

Whatever the rights or wrongs, as surely as night follows day, things went from bad to worse for both sides in the conflict because of their adherence to one part of the Declaration of Independence, and not the other. A horrible sense of foreboding pervaded the Land of the Free. American optimism turned into gloom and pessimism; the seventy-five thousand Lincoln volunteers needed by the Union to quell the revolt, turned into a recruitment of two and a half million. For the South it became one million.

To Europeans it appeared as utter madness. Not even Napoleon had raised armies that large. The lesson of Solferino was that any army in excess of 100,000 at any one battle was unmanageable, and that the inevitable losses were colossal.

*

It is with some regret that Olive Vanya arrived in Boston on a foggy late July morning, for it was cold and damp, and not what she expected. She had been told that New England in the Fall was one of the glorious sights of America, and that in the summer, as it was now, the climate was very European, but all she could see was a few large white mansion houses looming out of the mist. It was not inviting, the harbour had a smell to it, and there was wharf upon wharf of rotten wooden hulks, used for whaling. It was the world of *Moby Dick*; she felt like facing around, and sailing back to Europe there and then.

Then Olive was struck with the ludicrous nature of her fear, the folly of being frightened by the unknown. She faced the sight of Boston wilfully, and contented herself with putting her hands over her mouth to keep out the smell, and remained on deck to survey the scene. There, besides her, was the Admiral, a little old withered man, brown, succinct, and fiery, who had got on board at the Azores. He wore an old fashioned naval uniform of blue, faced with white, which set off his mahogany face of a thousand deep wrinkles, so that he looked as though he had been tattooed by life. At his side stood a tall, large-boned, masculine, middle-aged woman like a man in petticoats. There was a touch of brogue in her looks, her face of rouge and powder could not conceal that she was anything other than Irish.

She was the Admiral's wife, and Olive was hoping that this would be the last she saw of them, for they had told her, despite her faltering English, the whole history of the Admiral's life and adventures. In normal circumstances, if he had been a General, it might have been interesting, but as an Admiral, he had spent his whole life at sea.

The Admiral had come into life sixty five years before in the middle of Chesapeake Bay while his mother was taking a little trip from Norfolk to Annapolis on board her husband's flag ship (he too, had been an admiral), when rather before he was expected, the admiral was born. This had fixed his destiny. At the age of twelve he had gone to sea and had remained there ever since, until now when an unlucky war promotion was sending him ashore, and seemed likely to keep him there. (Olive assumed it was for the Union side, but she was not certain). During the Atlantic crossing, he had been a little testy, and addicted to making others tipsy while he remained sober; besides this he had a few prejudices incident to his condition, a loathing of the rest of the world, particularly Spaniards and Mexicans. This was in part due to service in the Gulf of Mexico and around the islands in the Caribbean Sea, for its there that he had seen much of his early action. He also had a dislike for the English, partly because of the War with them in '12 in which he served under Perry; partly because his wife was Irish, and the English were scoundrels to them.

As for the admiral's wife, she thoroughly understood her despotic husband's nature, and her happier disposition had enabled her to conform to it without any appearance of reluctance or discontent. The admiral having reached the age of forty without the slightest compunction to marry, had, during a sojourn in Cork harbour, fallen in love with her. Then a buxom widow, he had married her in something less than three weeks. Though course and boisterous, she was heartily hospitable, good humoured, and incorruptibly maternal. Having had no children of her own, she and the Admiral were brooding to be grandparents to anyone's children. The years at sea had given them much, but very little to keep them on shore.

During the voyage, the admiral and his wife had taken to Olive as if she was their own daughter, and on finding out she was a widow, they had firmly decided to find her a husband as soon as they arrived in Boston. She was to come and stay with them, there was no question of it, for the navy had supplied them with a large sprawling house which they had not yet seen, and she was to make herself at home with them until a good Irish-American boy could be found for her.

Olive thanked them for her offer, but told them that she was already engaged to another in Boston so as not to offend them. When they had asked her for his name, thinking of one of her letters, she had said Mr. Henry James. They had been thoroughly disappointed, for they had never heard of him, which was a relief to Olive, for all she knew, he might have been married.

17

The War had gone beyond the ninety days expected by Henry James, Senior. The

North had lost the battle of Bull Run and fallen back on Washington D.C. The day after, he had received a letter at his home in Newport from a young European countess accompanied by the letter of introduction from Bill Howells. In her letter, she stated that she was in Boston, and would be honoured to meet him. Without telling anyone, he had taken a boat out of the long pier and gone to Boston.

"Mam, I am honoured to meet you. Young Howells wrote to me about you." He had met Howells the previous summer in New York. Howells had introduced himself to Waldo Emerson, who in turn had introduced him to Henry. Henry in turn had introduced him to his sons, and it was they, more than the father, who had befriended Bill. "Bill is a friend of our literary family." The literary family included Nathaniel Hawthorne and Washington Irvine.

Henry James Snr. walked with a limp. He had been taking part in an outdoor chemistry experiment at Albany Academy when he was thirteen, igniting small paper balloons fuelled by turpentine, when one set fire to a hayloft. He had attempted to stamp out the flames, but his right leg had caught fire, and had to be amputated below the knee. After four years in hospital, and further amputation above the knee, he had gone through the rest of life on a wooden leg.

"It is gracious for you to meet me, Mister James." Olive pronounced Mister as though it was a title like Count or Prince, and James, a man who had turned from gambling, drink, debt, and agreed to settle down, the sound of the pretty girl from Austria calling him Mister so reverently, melted his wicked old heart.

"I have been to Europe countless times" he smiled. He had an eye for feminine beauty, and an eagerness for female company. "When I got your handwritten note, the handwriting told me that you would be young, beautiful and charming. The perfume re-affirmed it."

Olive ensconced herself in a fine Boston hotel in Cambridge. The one recommended by William Howells, the Astor, had not been agreeable to her - it had been full of miscreants in search of gratification of all kinds - so a selective Cambridge hotel had been suggested to her, and she had found it to her liking.

"Thank you for the compliment, Mister James."

"Call me, Henry." He was all of fifty, but in the presence of Olive, he felt twenty again. "Can I call you, Olive? This is America, and we don't like to stand on ceremony here."

She conceded his request with a little nod to the side, which due to the differences in culture, he took to mean no, for she had still not mastered American sign language. It was very confusing. "I mean yes, not no" she laughed not knowing which way to tilt her head.

Henry laughed too. "In America, Olive, sometimes a man says yes when he means no. We all get confused in this country. People lie all the time." Henry had written a long series of works on religion, most of which tried to explain the relationship between God and man. In his writings he tried to apply his religious ideas to the social and political issues of the day. "My father was an Irish peasant immigrant who became a multi-millionaire and he died bitter and twisted. I wasn't going to let that happen to me. He cheated and lied his way through life."

Olive was wondering where the conversation would lead, but then again, what difference did it make what people talked about, deep down they were all lonely, all reaching out, all being driven by the same motives of self-interest and personal gratification.

"He is dead?" she asked out of politeness, more than out of interest.

"Dead as a cow on the end of a meat hook. I was overjoyed. See, my father left his three million dollars in trust for mother, myself and the other children. It wasn't a case of waiting until we were twenty-one, damn no, we had to prove to the trustees by living another twenty one years that we were sound upright citizens who contributed to society. My mother could hardly afford to keep the house on what we received for a living allowance in the meanwhile. We contested the will for eleven years before we got a settlement. My share of the interest money came to ten thousand dollars a year."

Olive had never heard people talk about their finances so openly. It seemed to be a point of honour amongst Americans to declare their annual income. Olive did not know if ten thousand dollars a year was a lot or not. She herself had arrived in Boston with about fifty thousand dollars. She had not thought it much.

"Who can live on ten thousand dollars a year nowadays?" he asked her. "But then, twenty years ago, it was a fortune to a young single man. I went to Ireland and England, took with me my own personal tutor, and a black servant ... like some American circus, we ate gooseberries with my Irish cousins. Oh, there was one," his eyes went misty "a certain beauty called Barbara ... she was everything I ever wanted in life, but she was engaged. Then I found Sandeman, a Scotsman who advocated a simple relationship between God and man. I returned to live in New York, using his books to start a publishing venture. My aim was to expose the current church systems as narrow, corrupt, and un-Christian." His face shone with zealousness. "I had this romantic notion that the ways of nature and of the spirit were ultimately one. I was determined to work on a large-scale reinterpretation of the Bible in which the scripture would be revealed to function symbolically rather than literally."

As they sat having pink lemonade in the breakfast room of the hotel, Olive found herself completely lost. She could not follow Henry at all. Her English was only good enough to order or ask for things. She understood the language better than she could speak it, but the New England drawl and length of the words used by the middle-aged man, completely baffled her.

However, as in Vienna, she had learned that saying nothing, smiling from time to time, and fixing her attention on the speaker, switching her gaze from the mouth, to the hands, to the eyes, was a successful counter to ignorance. It was with such tactics she followed the conversation of Henry James, listening for key words that might allow her to interrupt and show she understood the drift of his monologue.

"Then I got married." A sudden twitch seemed to go down his right leg, for he shifted uncomfortably, and moved his wooden leg with both hands.

"You have children, Henry?" Olive had seized on the word wife.

"Four sons and a daughter... and proud I am of them." He had hoped not to bring his family into the conversation. "I didn't let that stop me from travelling. We went to live in Europe twice. In Windsor, England in '44 and '45, and in '55, Geneva, Paris, London, then back to Paris until '58. I speak very good French."

The mention of this prompted Olive to ask Henry if they could switch to speaking French as she had learned French in Vienna. He was delighted, but as soon as he began to do so, she realised that his French was street French, and her's society French, to the extent that she was just as confused as ever when he spoke.

"Do you know Paris, Olive?" She said she did not. "I tried to take the family back there in '59, went as far as booking passage on the *Persia*, but I met such a resistance from friends and family, I postponed the journey. But in the end, I triumphed, we spent the winter in Geneva and Frankfurt-on-Maine. However, my German is not very good, and that is why I haven't mentioned it until now, for you English is far superior."

She tried to coax him into conversation, but he would not speak German, though she was certain his understanding of the language was good.

"My sons speak excellent German. See, Olive that is why I went to Europe, to educate my children, to send them to the best schools in Paris and Geneva. What is a boy without education?" He thought briefly about his own education at Albany Academy and Princeton Theological Seminary. "Young boys are running away from college to join the volunteers. I won't let Willy and Harry go." William was twenty, Henry Jnr. eighteen. "No young American should put himself in the way of death until he has realised something good in life ... until he has found some charming conjugal or other woman to whisper his devotions to." Henry looked straight at Olive. Perhaps she was the sort of woman who could keep his sons from thinking about joining Lincoln's army. He had no doubt that one of them would fall in love with her; she was overwhelmingly beautiful. She would be the lure by which he would keep them at home. Henry wished that he were young again. His own experience of life had taught him that men were born to have and pursue lurid sexual thoughts. If it were not for marriage, there would be no salvation. Yet, he delighted in the excitement of being in a woman's company. As for his sons, he could put up with their puerile, overheard, dinner table curses of 'May his mashed potatoes always have lumps in them!', if it meant he could keep them out of the damned war. To Henry James Snr., the ideas of government were not worth an honest human life. The loss of his own leg had given him the equivalent of a war wound; he knew that such sacrifice would be a handicap after the war.

"Would you like to be my guest in Newport? We have a big old house. Wilky can room up with Bob."

"Perhaps when I return from Washington. I received notice from President Lincoln today."

"President Lincoln!!!" Henry James moved his leg with his hands as if the pain had become unbearable. "What does that old bird want?"

"He wants to meet me" Olive replied timidly.

"He's in the middle of a war!" Henry was upset. He could see his plans coming to nothing. By the time Olive was back from Washington, his son's would be in the Volunteers. "I have a fear that man has a greater commitment to preserving the Union than freeing the slaves." He had once been a mild democrat, and though he was now an advocate of the newly formed Republicans (though, his father was an Irish immigrant, he was American), he had begun to see Abraham Lincoln's flaws. "You tell that man I voted for - if he doesn't finish the war, it will finish him."

Henry ordered some drinks, alcoholic ones. "You tried Bourbon, Olive?" The black waiter brought the drinks in two large whisky glasses. "This will give you a taste of America." He threw his head back and swallowed it all in a gulp. Olive did the same. "Two more" he ordered. The waiter went away quickly. "Now, Olive, you've heard all about me ... now, I want to hear all about you."

Olive began her story, for now that she was in the Land of the Free, it seemed that her Cinderella history was the type of story Henry James might want to hear. America revelled in rag to riches tales, and everyone had one to tell. So she recounted her own, beginning with her birth as a Russian peasant....

18

Olive's trip to Washington was a nightmare. At one point it was halted in Philadelphia when news came through that the Rebs had marched up Washington's Dolly Madison Boulevard, but official reports denied it. No one really knew what was going on.

Olive was not alone, she was accompanied by Alice James, Henry's daughter, for he would not allow her to make the journey to Washington alone. Alice was two weeks short of her thirteenth birthday; behind her were the broken years of living in Europe; a mish-mash of Atlantic crossings; an assortment of maids and tutors; and a future as her self-indulgent father's crutch in old-age.

Alice did not find it easy to make friends. She had a sharp tongue and was highly strung. She had a plain broad-face, a high brow, straight brown hair that she braided, grey eyes, and a complexion that was sallow. When nervous she trembled violently, cried, screamed, developed headaches, refused to eat. When her father had first told her that she was going to Washington with a foreign countess, she had behaved like a spoiled brat.

"I wanted to throw myself out of the window, or knock father's head off as he sat with his silver locks at the dinner table ... but I'm glad I didn't." She enjoyed being with Olive more than anything she had ever done in her life before. "I am insane, father and mother say so."

Olive looked at the pre-pubescent girl and saw the weight of the James house resting on her shoulders. "It is the duties of doctor and nurse your papa places on you, Cherie" said Olive putting her arm around her shoulders. The girl needed love. "Your father expects too much of you."

This was the truth of the matter. Alice's brain had been overloaded by reading books, resulting in a broken education, fragmented to the extent that it had scattered her brain. She did not want to spend the rest of her childhood being tutored at home; she wanted to attend a proper school like her brothers. Olive identified with Alice's desire to be with girls of her own age, for she herself had been denied that, first in Constantinople, then in

Vienna, until Franz had taken her to the Conservatory class of his sister-in-law Anna Frohlich.

Delayed in Philadelphia, Olive made enquiries, then arranged to take Alice to visit the Normal School, where young women were educated to become teachers. It was a hope that Alice might like the school, and if so, that her father might allow her to enrol. It was a thought, for Olive recognised that Alice needed to get out and experience more of life.

The classrooms of the Normal School were fully occupied, and the principal herself showed them around. The fact that the principal was a woman surprised Olive.

"Our school is open to all classes". She pointed to two girls, sitting side by side. "One is the daughter of a millionaire, and the other's mother supports herself by washing." Alice shifted uncomfortably at the idea, for she knew her father would not like that, and had heard him say so. In his view, daughters should be sent to private boarding school or have governesses at home. "Here, our young women are taught physiology" she said showing them another class where young women were learning about cartilages and tissues. "And here, mathematics. Our present lecturer is also a pupil here."

The young woman teacher momentarily halted, said good-day, as did all the pupils in every class they entered, then continued. "And here, our ladies are learning composition." The Principal urged them to take a seat at the back of the classroom.

Olive was amused. She had never been in a classroom in her life before. It was full of giggling girls, whispering and turning to look at the strangers at the back of the room. At the front was a fourteen year old girl who read aloud a letter she had written on an imaginary subject - in this instance a picnic by the Delaware River.

The teacher asked for criticisms. "Can any one point out any faults of expression or grammar in the letter that has just been read?"

"I think" answered one of class "that one sentence was not quite clear. I am uncertain whether it was the tart or the grass that was eaten at the picnic."

This produced a lot of merriment, and so the ball kept rolling, so to speak, until all the faults had been exposed, and the girl's classmates were inclined to reduce her letter to a joke.

The teacher called for order, and the Principal thanked the girls for their thoroughly exhaustive examination of the letter before the girl who penned it burst into tears.

Olive and Alice were shown the teaching of drawing, music and song, after which they were invited to lunch. After the break, the entire school of three hundred was assembled in the main hall, and with a sudden shock, Olive was asked to address them. Alice looked askance, and moved her seat back slightly to be in the shadows, fearful that they might ask her to speak too.

"Thank you, Madam." said Olive to the

principal as the clapping subsided. How could she refuse? As a singer she had been used to audiences of eight or nine hundred in Vienna, but she had sung in German and Italian, not spoken in English. "Girls, I must ask you to look at the other girls by your side and ask this one simple question. What do you want from life? I began life very humbly and I expected nothing from it. It is by chance that I rose to be an opera singer and Countess. Some say that it is my looks that enabled me to do so, and I do not deny that they have helped. But more than anything else, it has been my will to learn, and my desire to discover the secrets of life that have propelled me. I have had to learn five languages which are not my own, and I have had at every turn to adapt and take life as it comes. There are those who say that life is pre-determined, and there are others who profess that life is what we make it. I subscribe to the notion that it is a combination of both, that our education prepares us for the pre-destined, and that through personal knowledge we learn that our education is never complete. What I have seen today in your school is the future, that tutors and home-education, once only the preserve of the wealthy, will become a thing of past, and that all mankind, women as well as men, will benefit from universal education. I applaud the achievements of this school, and wish that in my own younger days that I had had the opportunity to study in a school such as this in Russia."

The mention of Russia cued the Principal

from her seat. She led the school in a rapturous ovation, thanking their speaker. "We hope, Countess, that your invigorating speech will encourage your ward Miss James to come and join us in the new term." Alice went bright red. "Her father, school, is the great Boston theologian Henry James, a leading light in the cause of emancipation of the slaves, and I know he believes equally as strong in the emancipation of woman." A great cheer went up. "To your classes now."

The assembly dispersed, and as the Principal saw Olive and Alice to the gates of the school, she had some final words for Olive. "I hope you will tell President Lincoln that Philadelphia Normal School is one hundred percent for the Union." It was a patriotic statement, an indication that the Principal cared for her country and upheld its ideals despite the difficulties, for there was a general state of alarm in Philadelphia; the Rebs were getting close instead of being driven back to Richmond. No-one thought that there would be any fighting in Pennsylvania, but as the months went on, the war came closer and closer to spilling out of Virginia.

They travelled back by carriage to their hotel. "Would you like to go to school there?" Olive questioned Alice.

"No way" snapped Alice curtly.

"Nor would I" replied Olive with a gentle sigh and a smile. "Too much mathematic and not enough singing."

*

The train to Washington was full of troops. It was anything but comfortable. There was much more noise and shaking than all seemed necessary. Normally each car would contain fifty people, with a passage in the middle, to allow anyone who liked to pass from one car to another if they wished. Instead, the aisles were jammed with soldiers in blue course-cotton uniforms, many of them young boys of sixteen and seventeen, who had lied about their age so they could enlist. They were happy go-lucky, many chewed tobacco, which they would spit out the window. They joked that they would send the Rebs running all the way to Cuba, or when they got their hands on them, they would treat them like niggers, or that good old Abe would give them a medal for saving the White House. But as the train shuddered and halted, jolted on and halted, started again and halted, until there was endless delay, a frustration built up which produced endless curses from the soldiers. Eventually the soldiers fell quiet, some slept on their feet, others read books, wrote letters, played cards, but the majority just stared out the window, chewing their tobacco, thinking of home.

Olive and Alice were seated in the drawing-room car. Opposite them, two officers - a colonel and a major. For a long time no-one spoke, until the colonel whispered in the major's ear.

"Excuse me, ladies" the Major said touching the brim of his hat "Colonel Sherman would like to know if it is alright for him to light up a cigar?"

Olive and Alice both looked to the colonel. He was clean-shaven, fair-haired, blue eyed, sharp featured, and long-legged, as if he had been on a horse all of his life. He was not much older than thirty-five.

Olive nodded her approval. They were soldiers; tomorrow they could be dead. The uniforms of the officers were covered in yellow braid, but to Olive's eye, the material of their tunics was course like the regular soldiers. The American army had none of the glitter of the Austrian Imperial troops, but they looked like fighting men, not men ready for parade.

The colonel lit his cigar. Nothing more was said. Olive looked out the window, amazed that the train passed not only through towns but also along the streets of the towns without any guard or fence of any kind. She saw pigs trotting about the line, and later, a cow strayed on to the line, halting the train. For the Americans, it all seemed to be taken as a matter of course.

A conductor approached "I'm sorry, sir" he said most curtly "you can't smoke here."

The colonel looked up at the conductor with a glare that looked as though he might kill him. The major tapped him on the arm and drew his attention to Olive and Alice.

"Excuse me, kindly" spoke the Colonel as he rose to his full six feet and stood over the conductor, a little man in his fifties. He blew his cigar smoke into the conductor's face, and then pressed a silver dollar into his sweaty palm. Just then an itinerant musician entered the carriage playing a fiddle. The conductor put the dollar in the watch-pocket of his waistcoat and went off to chase the fiddle-player back up the train. The colonel sat down again. He finished his cigar, then settled down to sleep.

The Major read a book - *Walden* by Henry David Thoreau, an account of hermit-life in the woods in a hut built by the author's own hands, a man who declared that government is best which governs not at all. Alice shuffled in her seat. She looked pale and sickly. Olive took her in her arms and let her sleep on her lap, and watched the Major turn another page of wilderness.

*

In Washington, Olive had her meeting with the President at the White House at noon. Alice was very poorly after the train journey; she had taken one of her fits of temper and refused to visit the White House. Olive at a loss left her with her maid.

What maid?

It is a fact, that throughout history, the world has concerned itself with the lives and exploits of the rich and famous. It is rare that a reader of history wishes to dwell for long on the lives of the servants rather than the mistresses and masters. Perhaps the odd insight here and there is sufficient to understand the behind-doors goings-on, but it is an exception when the life of the servant is viewed as more important than the life of the one served. Perhaps, in a society that is trying to come to terms with a new liberalism or a new constitution that promotes equality, the life of the servant is more rigorously scrutinised than the life of the mistress or master. Certainly, there is merit in promoting the study of such worthy lives, but as we are in a conservative age, we shall not dwell long on Olive Vanya's maid.

*

Clarissa Blum was Viennese born and taken into domestic service by Marie Festetics when she was ten. When she was fourteen she was assigned to Olive as her personal maid, and for seven years had devoted herself to the well being of her mistress. She had gone to Madeira with her, and sailed with her from Venice to Boston. She accompanied her mistress almost everywhere. She had no opinions, was not very good looking, and wherever she went with her mistress, she remained unobtrusive to the extent that no one ever noticed her presence.

*

Nothing could have been less formal than a White House reception. Olive arrived in all her American finery bought in Boston - a hundred dollar coat; sixty dollar dress; twenty-five dollar silk umbrella; five dollar pair of gloves. The hire of a luxury carriage cost her three dollars an hour.

To her shock, in the ante-rooms, Olive found herself waiting with men in shooting coats, mud splattered uniforms, and long-tail coats that looked as though they had been used as blankets. The group of six women were no better dressed in their calicos and cottons; all without coats, but with a mind to their umbrellas or fans, which they twirled and shook as the talked. Their voices carried up into the high ceilings of the White House, and Olive could not fail to compare the impressive scale of the boulevards and avenues and government buildings outside, with the modest dimensions of the Presidents residence inside. It was not the Hofburg, but there was a freshness about it that made her feel that the American nation of thirty-one millions was not weighed down by centuries of bad government and autocratic rulers.

Olive was admitted into the presence of the President along with the half dozen ladies. One of the ladies was a strong-minded woman whose hobby was education. She immediately attacked the President on the subject and monopolised his attention for a full quarter of an hour while giving him her peculiar views. Most patiently, Abraham Lincoln listened with a quiet smile on his lips, now and then interposing a remark that showed that he had a sense of humour. The ladies were shown out.

'You pay dearly for high office, Mr. President ...' thought Olive. She could see by the tiredness of the President's eyes that he was compelled to forebear many such remarks. He had a full and heavy countenance, and the firmness that he had displayed in the face of national disaster in his five months as president, was legibly written on his face. He looked dismayed. His beard, jet black at his election, was quickly turning white. As the son of an illiterate and wandering frontier family, he had become a storekeeper in New Salem, Illinois, then a postmaster, a lawyer, a Whig congressman, then back to obscurity. Seven years later, he joined the new Republicans and ran for senate, unsuccessfully. Then by chance, he was in the right place at the right time to secure the Republican nomination for president, and ran on a slavery containment ticket. He won because the democrats were divided and ran two candidates - Breckenridge and Douglas. It was his fate to be the sixteenth president of the United States. He did not look as though he was enjoying it. He looked fumbling and indecisive.

Lincoln slumped in his chair. It all seemed to be too much for him. It was he alone who was responsible for the war, and it was to him they looked to end it. He rested his head in his right hand.

Olive watched him. She had become unnoticed, sitting a little at the back of the room against the curved walls. Mr. Lincoln sat behind his desk, the light streaming in behind him, falling on his back, illuminating him like some angel from heaven.

Olive sat perfectly still, she did not want to disturb the moment, the first quiet moment of the day, by all appearances, the president's too. The sun was still on his rounded back, splattering across his long-tailed coat and scattering on to his thick grey hair. She wondered what drove a man to become the elected ruler of a nation. Franz Josef had had no choice, he had been born to it, but a man like Abraham Lincoln, a peasant who had risen to the highest office of the land, surely this was what was known as the American Dream.

Yet, sitting there, the man was living out his worst nightmares. Who in their right mind would relish the responsibility of President of the Untied States? Its citizens were freethinking, free spoken, and forthright to the extent that any action immediately stimulated opposition from somebody, about something, over something else. The man who was president could never hope to change the nation; he could only hope that the fibre of the nation was not worse when he left office than when he took it up. As for the morals of the nation, that was not the president's concern. Freedom of religion allowed each American to set his or her own morals. The President was not expected to be a preacher, a spokesperson for God. Unlike the Emperor of Austria, he was human, he was accountable, he was allowed to show his feelings; he got four years of hell in office, so that afterwards he could live the rest of his life in paradise.

Lincoln looked up. He had remembered that he was not alone. He saw the young woman sitting quietly at the other end of the room. A secretary whispered in his ear. Suddenly his eyes brightened; he rose; he walked across the room. Olive saw him speeding towards her and managed to rise just as he offered his hand.

"My, you're so young, my daughter's age" he declared with an admiring look. "I thought you would be well past it, some old spinster. Come, lets go into the garden, I need some fresh air."

He led her into the rose garden. "Isn't it beautiful? You should see it in the Spring." Many of the petals of the rose bushes had dropped in the summer heat, but there were still enough in bloom to scent the whole garden. It reminded Olive of the day she had first met Sisi and rode after her into the Laxenberg grounds. "Come, dear, tell me all about the Empress Elizabeth. Is she really as beautiful as her photographs and portraits convey?"

Olive proceeded to tell the President everything he wanted to know about Sisi - how, yes, it was true that she was even more beautiful in real life, and that her personality matched her beauty, and that it was shame she was married to Franz Josef.

At this information, Abraham raised his eyebrows, for as a congregator like Henry James, he was a stickler for proper behaviour between man and wife. Olive put his mind at rest, saying that it was not Franz Josef that was the problem, but the Empire. The duties put upon him as the ruler of seventy millions was so onerous, his relationship with his wife suffered.

The statement seemed to strike a chord with Mr. Lincoln. "I've been with Mrs. Lincoln too many years now to let the presidency come between us, but I could see that a young couple with fifty or sixty years ahead of them as sole rulers, might suffer considerably for the good of their nation. I'm not even six months into my term and I can appreciate the pressures. At first it is easy to take on the work load, to make decisions, give orders, but as time goes by, I begin to question if I am making the right decisions, giving the right orders. Worse than that, I'm not sure if the aides who helped me to get into the White House are the right aides to see me through my term. Too often I leave a decision to one of my team, and they fail me. I am judged by their failure, to the extent that any decision should be my decision, so increasing all decisions are made by me. This increases my workload, I have less time to make each decision, so in the end I make more bad decisions." He looked up at the sky. "I miss the backwoods."

The President took Olive tightly by the arm and led her down to the bottom of the garden so that he could talk to her about the architecture of the House. It was indeed splendid, reminiscent of the architecture she had seen in Italy. "The real reason I asked to see you was whether you could help America. Franz Joseph's brother has been offered the title of Emperor of Mexico. Is he a threat to the Union?"

Olive did not honestly know. Emperor of Mexico? She knew the nature of Max Ferdinand. "I need not think you should worry about Max, Mr. President."

"But what if his brother helps him to try and reclaim the lands Mexico has ceded to America?"

Again, Olive did not know the ins and outs of North American politics. "It is my experience that Franz Josef will be glad to see the back of his brother. He has been an embarrassment to him for some time."

"I see." Lincoln brooded for a moment. "So you don't think Maximillan will supply the South with troops against us?"

"No" Olive asked plainly. Maximillan, like so many other Austrians, was a toy soldier.

"Thank you, Countess" Lincoln seemed pleased. They fell into idle chat for a few minutes. He was captivated by her beauty, she by his power.

Then, just as he was taking her arm and walking her back towards the House, a little man came running out waving a piece of paper. He spoke swiftly to the President, and then went running back into the House.

"I am so sorry. I must leave you now. I have enjoyed our conversation immensely. It is so rare that I get to speak my own mind these days. Please write to me if you require anything during your stay in America. I shall be delighted to help." He shook her hand. "Stay in the garden as long as you wish. I will send someone out to take you back to the main entrance. Goodbye and God bless." He turned and strode swiftly back to his office. Through the windows Olive could see a gathering of blue-uniformed military men with lots of yellow braid. They were earnestly discussing something, and she could hear raised voices.

A black servant came out and led her back to her hired carriage that was drawn up outside the main entrance. She was helped into the carriage; the door closed behind her. The driver coaxed his two horses to walk, and within a minute they were out on to Pennsylvania Avenue and trotting along past the government buildings and back towards the hotel where Clarissa was tending Alice.

19

When Olive took Alice back to the James's in Newport she was given news that totally shocked her.

Grigori was alive!

"I cannot believe it", she uttered with a dry throat. "He died at Solferino. It was all a mistake, and he was shot ...". She had been taken by Mrs. James and Clarissa and placed in an armchair.

"It's true alright", boomed Henry James. "My boys met him in Geneva while I was in Frankfurt." Henry had been talking to William and Henry Jnr. and they had spoken of meeting the Count Rostov at an American embassy party the previous year. "Young Harry will tell you himself."

An eighteen year old boy came into Olive's view from behind her armchair. He was slim, good-looking, dark haired, of medium height with sharp grey eyes like his father's. In his face was a stubborn and persistently wilful look. His hair was parted on the left, and from the expanse of forehead already exposed, his hair had begun to recede almost before he was a man. His clothes had a European cut, a waistcoat of dark cloth that closely fitted the contours of his torso, tapering into a pair of light breeches. He stood with his head slightly tilted to the left, almost as if it were too heavy to hold upright, for it was one of those round heads that has the tendency to roll and pitch, never allowed rest, always thrown this way or that by the forces of life acting upon it.

"It is true, Countess" Henry Jnr. stated in a high effeminate voice "Willy and I were invited to a party at the embassy and there we met a man who called himself the Count Rostov."

"What did he look like? How did he look?" Olive wanted to know everything, for although she knew Grigori to be dead, in her heart he lived.

"Well, he looked kind of funny ..." Henry saw the stern look of his father, and corrected himself "I mean, I suppose he looked Russian. He was certainly different looking from anyone else there. He was massive ... I mean, he was very tall and so well built that I think he must have been the strongest man in the room. He moved like a dancer, and I could not keep my eyes off him, he was so graceful. I pointed him out to Willy, so Willy, one for pushing himself forward, went over and introduced himself. They chatted for a little while, laughed at some things, and from his laughter, I sensed he was a nice fellow." Henry Jnr. stole a glance at his father. He was not sure if he was being polite enough, for there had been a few things in the Count's demeanour he had not liked, in particular his arrogance with the embassy servants.

"Go on, Henry!" Alice was impatient to find

out if it was the real Count Rostov or not.

"Well, if Willy was here he could tell you for himself what was spoken between them." Henry's memory was excellent, it had just become family habit that he always deferred himself to his elder brother who had just gone up to Cambridge to study science at Harvard. The decision had only just been made. Until the week before, Willy having been inspired by the Louvre, had been studying painting at Hunt's studio. Now, to the utter delight of their father, he had denounced art and found refuge in science. "They talked about art and that sort of stuff, then finally got around to talking about why the Count was in Geneva. It seems that the Csar is almost bankrupt and wants to sell land. Willy asked him what land he was talking about, and the Count replied that the Csar was considering selling the territory of Alaska to anyone who could come up with the money. Hence his presence in the American embassy, for the Csar is reluctant to sell to the French or British as they're too powerful."

"Are you sure it was Grigori Shum, Count Rostov your brother was talking to?" Olive had to interrupt. The sale of land did not interest her. "How old was he?"

"Hard to say ... maybe forty, a little less. I would have thought him young except that the lines on his face showed his age. I found that out when Willy introduced me to him."

"You met him then???" Olive could not stop her voice rising. For the last two years she had believed Grigori to be dead. Now, there before her in a house in Massachusetts was a young man who was saying that he had spoken to the husband.

"Sure" said Henry Jnr. matter-of-factly. "I want to be an author like Bill Howell. If I don't meet people I won't have anything to write." He ended his sentence with a smile, trying to hide his own motives and to conceal from his parents his true feelings, that, he had been attracted by Grigori, and having butted in on his brother's conversation, had introduced himself to the Count. "We talked about the Red Cross."

"What's that, Henry" Mrs. James enquired.

"It's a new organisation set up to help wounded soldiers, Mother" Henry replied. "After the battle of Solferino, a Swiss businessman called Dunant coaxed the women of the town to nurse and supply bandages, children to carry water, and anyone else who happened to be there to help the wounded. The Count told me" continued Henry Jnr. "that he had been in a bed for five weeks with rifle wounds in Solferino, and had it not been for Dunant, he said he would have died. He unbuttoned his shirt and showed us where three bullets had gone through his chest. He also pointed to a scar on the side of his right forehead where a bullet had gone into his skull. It was then that I noticed that his left arm was missing below the elbow."

"You mean he had lost an arm?" Olive was almost in tears.

"Not only that, Countess ..." Henry Jnr. paused. He was not sure if he could tell her so soon after the arm, but he decided that it was best to tell all and have it done with all in one go. "He had also lost his sight. He was blind."

Olive broke into tears. Alice, Henry Jnr., and Henry Snr. were sent out the room. Mary James and Clarissa did all they could to comfort the heart-broken countess, for the shock had been too much, first to learn that Grigori was alive, but secondly to discover that he was no longer the Grigori of old.

They fetched blankets and brought out a folding bed for her to lie on, and once she was asleep, the entire James family discussed with Clarissa how they could arrange to unite the Countess with her estranged husband.

20

Six weeks after the news, Olive Vanya re-crossed the Atlantic. She had lost a lot of weight and had continuous pins and needles in her fingers and toes. From the moment she had found out Grigori was alive she had become fatigued and weak. She had a constant need for liquids and had become easily irritated. She complained of blurred vision and had a permanent cold. The James's doctor had put her on a diet of high-fibre and advised her to eat raw garlic. On no account was she to eat foods with sugar.

The James's had made contact with their friends in Geneva, and after some time, with the help of a private investigator, they had traced the Count, first to London, then to Manchester, where he had Russian friends. It was discovered that from there he had gone to Liverpool and crossed the Irish Sea to Dublin. Further investigation revealed that he had retired to the west, and that he was in Connaught. Local folk in the area of Benbulbin in Sligo had confirmed to the investigator that a man calling himself Grigori Shum, Count Rostov, had taken up residence there.

*

On a cold October morning, Olive disembarked on to the quay in Galway harbour. It had been a terrible Atlantic crossing, and Olive had been sick much of the journey, but as soon as she stepped onto Irish soil, she made immediate enquires for the onward journey to County Sligo.

Clarissa could not control her mistress, she had done her best to humour her and steer her from bad company on board the ship, but now that they were on land, she felt that her mistress would drive herself too hard and make herself worse. She wanted to rest for a day or two in Galway, but Olive instructed a carriage driver to take them to the station immediately.

Three car drivers with their whips slung over the shoulders stood by the station gate as they arrived. Olive and Clarissa pushed past the beggars and boarded a train for Sligo.

"Apples, or'nges - buy a cake" called out a bare-footed woman toiling along the platform. Two constables in trim dark-green uniforms and bayonets at their sides, patrolled the platform, giving a quick glance into each compartment as they strode. Bare-legged boys and girls, young women in red petticoats and dark-blue hooded cloaks, old women in black cloaks and white-ribbon night-caps, old men in filthy tatters stripped off scarecrows, watched as the train prepared to leave.

The engine shrieked, and the carriages began to rattle out of Galway and into the bogs of Connaught, spreading on either side for miles and miles. Before long, the train lurched to a halt.

"Jessus ..." cried out a man with his head out the window "an engine's run aff at the crassin', so it 'as."

"H-which t'ats ye're sayin'" another asked his older friend "'Tis this engine is'it, or not?"

"'Tis another for sure. An' ye wouldn't run over the poor crathur either, would ye?" said the man with his head out the window. "The cow seems fine."

A carriage-less engine having jumped the rails had slid down the embankment. Everyone stuck their heads out their carriage window to have a look as they slowly trundled past it. The train gathered speed, and the air in the carriage became colder and colder.

"Do you mind if we close the windows" Olive coughed as they pulled out of Athenry.

"Not at all, at all" said the older of the men. They were priests. To Olive the priests seemed to be the only well-dressed people on the train. Their coats were glossy black, and unlike the priests in Austria, their eyes did not glide about with downcast or furtively glancing eyes as if to avoid insult, instead, they had a thoroughly homely look which struck Olive. The older priest joked paternally with the younger one about being compromised by sharing a carriage with two young ladies.

"To be sure, father" the younger one laughed "they'll not be trying to kiss us as long as the train is moving."

The priests departed at Claremorris and their places were taken by a man home from Australia to visit his family. He tried to make conversation about politics, but he soon gave up and fell to reading a copy of an illustrated magazine called Good Works.

They arrived in Sligo mid-afternoon and descended from the train. Clarissa paid a porter to carry the luggage to a carriage which would take them to the town's best hotel, but Olive would have none of it, she wanted to carry on to Drumcliff under Benbulbin there and then. Clarissa tried to reason with her mistress, but Olive would hear none of her excuses.

The carriage driver suggested they left their luggage at the hotel as the road to Drumcliff was as rough as any in Ireland. He said he would take them as far as he could without risking breaking his springs, thereafter they would have to walk.

"An Oi wouildn't be after wearing those clothes if Oi was goin' abroad under Benbulbin. Ye'll need warm wet wetter stuff, sure ye will." The cabbie was an old Siigo man "Oi'l take ye to the 'otel, an' ye can have a bite an' a change."

Olive admitted that their clothing was totally unsuitable for the outdoors. When they had left Boston it had been warm and sunny, but now in Ireland, there was the threat of rain and a damp breeze coming off the breakers in Sligo Bay.

They ate and changed at the Sligo Hotel. Olive had already begun to ask if anyone had seen the Count Rostov resident at Drumcliff, but none could say they had. She asked if there was a big house there, but again no-one could say, except the hotel porter, who said that there had once been a big house, in fact a castle, but that it was now a ruin. This perplexed Olive, for she began to think that perhaps the James's information was wrong and that Grigori was not in Ireland at all. Then an old woman, who cleaned the floors of the hotel, spoke:

"Oi be a Dartry Mountain woman, an' Oi've heard there's a man livin' in one of the ol' abandon cotter houses out on the bog."

"Oi 'erd that too" said the porter suddenly remembering. "OI'l bet it not be 'e ye'll be lookin' after, for sure."

Olive looked dismayed "We will find out soon enough."

The cabbie took directions from the old woman as Olive and Clarissa readied themselves for the journey. The weather was holding and there was three hours of light left.

"Now, Michael Cormack" warned the porter "ye'll not be leavin' these ladies, or Oi'll kill ye."

The cabbie smiled "Not at all, Joseph Cormack, Oi'll have them safe in me eye all the while. They be grand ladies, an' Oi've taken a likin' to them." He winked."Oi better be havin' a little dram for the road."

The porter produced a bottle of whiskey from a cupboard. "Chust the one now, brother Michael."

"Weel, Oi better be havin a big glass then, brother Joseph, for it's a long ride to the ol' castle an' up the glen."

The two brothers blessed their old mother and had barely drained their glasses when the two women presented themselves for the journey.

"Oi'll be tellin' ma to keep yer meal in the pot, bruther" the porter joked. "Good luck to ye, lassies."

Michael Cormack set his horse off at a canter and nearly rode over a wheeled dog-kennel in which an old woman sat knitting while being pushed by a young woman. "Get out me way, you dirty ol' beggars." He veered so violently, Olive was almost thrown out of the carriage, but Clarissa caught her by the elbow. "A thousan' forgivin's misses" he shouted back at them with a swivel of his head.

They carried on out of Sligo without further mishap. On the road they passed men who were mending it - men in high crowned hats, brass-buttoned frieze dress coats, corduroy breeches, and gaiters or blue stockings - spooning about the stones with handle-less shovels with hafts as long as hoes. They all doffed their hats as soon as they saw Olive and Clarissa.

"Is't a wedding yer going to Michael, tis it, with those fine women?" one of the men shouted after him as a joke.

The road soon began to deteriorate and they met an old man leading a horse coming the other way. The little horse was dragging a small cart with shafts that stuck out front as much as they did aft. It was laden with a roped load of turf covered with straw and furze. He gave a little wave, and passed on by.

Next, over a rise ahead, came a thirty-year old farmers bhoy in a ragged, caped, drab great-coat buttoned over a ragged shirt, a limpet shell hat hanging over his bearded face, and corduroy trousers with a Vandyked tattered fringe at his leg bottoms. Some way behind him came a roguish-eyed girl singing like a lark, bent beneath the weight of a basket of cabbages heaped high above her hooded head. Olive thought that she might be his wife, but Michael soon dispelled that idea.

"Chesus, Brendan Gill, 'ave ye not got rid of that tinker girl, yet" he said in the passing.

"At least Oi have me a lassie, Michael Cormack" the farmer's bhoy replied. Then he saw Olive and Clarissa, and shouted after "Begging yer pardon" in a most mild and sincere tone.

"For sure, yer a witch of a girl, Cathleen Brogan" Michael called to the girl as they passed. She put her thumb to her nose and stuck out her tongue at him.

"You seem to know everyone, cabbie" Olive said to him as they began to cross dark bog and stone-strewn pasture.

"It's me job, miss, it is" he replied, "Oi knows ha'f of Sligo, and the other ha'f knows me."

Out on the bog land, they first saw an old woman in a black cloak, then a short while after, a bare-legged girl with a red shawl over her head, standing motionless in the middle of a half-flooded little meadow, staring at the carriage as if she wondered what could have brought strangers to her out-of-the-way place.

Olive shivered. "It is ugly here" she uttered with despair, having to remind herself why she now found herself in such a desolate place.

The cabbie was offended, for after all, he was a man easily riled. "Now, that's a terrible thing to say about the land of the Oirish. Why, maybe yer own grandmother is better lookin' than yerself, but if she were not, then sure, ye'd not suffer any to spake against her, miss."

Olive apologised, for the cabbie was right, it was a foolish thing to complain about any land to those who lived on it, for they knew the shortcomings of their land better than any stranger.

They were now travelling along a ditch-like bog lane - its black mud, dark and damp, sticking to the wooden spokes of the wheels. Suddenly they were back in the open, and there to the left, Olive saw the whole of Sligo Bay and the swell of the Atlantic which they had only finished crossing that morning. America seemed so far away. In a short time she had come to realise that America was a land of possibility. Now, in Ireland, she understood why so many fled the poverty of Europe to seek a new life; in particular, she began to see why so many Irish had found their way to America. Parts of Ireland were as poor as Russia. Why this was so, she did not know.

"Look now" said Michael Cormack "there below is Drumcliff. Oi can see the ol' castle, there on the edge of the town."

'What town' thought Olive? All she could see were a few thatched huts and the old ruin.

They began the descent into Drumcliff Bay and were met coming the other way by a red-headed little boy leading a donkey loaded with turf. The boy was brandishing a switch of blackthorn that he was waving to and fro in a pretence fight with some imaginary foe. Behind him followed his mother with a young daughter trotting besides her. The girl was also playing - she had thrown her petticoat over her head to make a hood and was peeping out at the carriage coming towards her.

At length they came to Drumcliff, a collection of cotter's dwellings standing on a grassy, stony knoll of bog, not far from the sea. The first dwelling had blotches of green slime dankly staining its white walls. Its grass thatch stood on end like a crop of hay. The single, dim little window made it look as though the cottage had an eye. The lower roofed outhouse looked more habitable. Hens clucked and cocks crowed; geese waddled out the open cottage door followed by a pig, stopping to rub its shoulder against the doorpost. The entire east leeside of the cottage and half the front was stacked with piles of turf.

Michael Cormack descended from the cab. "Sure, this is as far as we can ride, lassies, we must need hoof the rest of it, so help me."

He assisted them out of the cab. In the tiny little yard before them, three cylindrical little ricks leant drunkenly all at different angles. A little way off, a plumper rick, with a pole sticking out its apex stood beside a broken down wall, the other side of which, two cows were chasing off a donkey encroaching on their feed, whilst a goat watched their tussle from the safety of an outcrop of rock. A few sheep were nibbling in rough pasture meadow strewn with huge boulders which had tumbled off Benbulbin, many of the smaller ones heaped in cairns upon which sat black-eyed rooks. A stiff wind rushed in from the Atlantic, rolling the waves against the shores of the bay. Seagulls circled and screamed over the waves where a half drowned habitation stood on the sands. All around the cottage was a jumble of furze still in bloom; spotted orange lichens; gate-posts without gates; hedge banks without hedges; and endless tumbled-down whinstone walls. Beyond, a path led to two ruined cottages, ivy growing out in bushy clumps from the gables. Further on, one inhabited hovel clung to a cliff side; another of whitewashed mud; two of unmortared stone, windowless, chimney-less, with nothing but a bank of earth for their back wall.

Olive looked out over the dreary bog, tussocked with rusty rushes and jaundiced grass; blotted with turf stacks, lined with dismal dykes weaving sluggishly between weeping banks of peat. She was appalled, for she had forgotten about the poverty of her own first years in the Ukraine. Surely it had not been as dismal as this?

It all was a shock to her. Ireland was part of England, the richest country in the world. She could not believe it, but her eyes told her she had to believe it. Why had Grigori come to such a place?

The cotter had watched the coming of the carriage and come out of his cottage. "Good day, sir" said the cotter to the cabbie. "And to ye, ladies." They dispensed with the formalities, and as was the custom, for it was cold upon the shore, he invited them into his cottage for some tea.

He was an old man, but inside, was his mother, a shrivelled old woman, huddled up nose and knees in a faded red cloak, gazing dreamily from her low stool at the meal-like ash of the fragrant turf fire. By her side was chubby little girl with a crop of matted curls sitting on her bare heels looking up at her great-grandmother's face in hope of hearing another fairy story.

Olive turned away, she could not bear to faced by her own past, for it was from a situation not unlike this that she had been sold into slavery by her uncle. She had never understood it - at the time her uncle had said that he was doing it for her and not for money - now, reminded of the poverty, at last she could see some reasoning behind her uncle's action. Ireland could send its children to America, but in Russia, the only option was to sell children into a better life.

"Oi be tinkin' ye be here to see him" said the old man after they had enquired about Grigori. "There were a fella' here weeks ago askin' for him" grinned the old cotter "but he wouldn't see him. Oi had to send him away." He puffed out his chest "My land, see" he explained, proud of his forty acres of peat and rock.

"Is he still here then?" Olive asked frantically."

"H-why, maybe 'e is, maybe 'e flew off with the gulls" he said obtusely. "Who's asking, h-anyway?"

"I'm his wife." The smoke of the peat fire caught in her throat and choked her words.

"H-well" replied the cotter in a catch of breath "H-why, ye'll not find Donal Duggan standin' in the way of man an' his wife."

The old man explained that a blind man had come to him some nine months before looking for a cottage to rent on the condition that no man was to be allowed to visit him. "H-well, OI'll keep my barghain with the blind man. He says to me 'no man', so no man it must be." He looked at the cabbie. "But, h-why, he says nothin' to me about a woman, did he now, ma?"

The old woman did not reply; she had reached that stage in life, as in some cases, when the body outlives the mind, leaving little more than a semblance of the person who once inhabited it.

Michael Cormack and Clarissa agreed to

stay with the old woman and the young girl while Donal took Olive to the cottage of the blind man. He warned her that he was want to fits of rage and temper that had increased ten fold since he had first arrived. He said it was due to a bullet wound that the blind man had received in the head, and that part of the bullet, still lodged in his brain, was slowly killing him.

Olive accepted the bad news. This was Grigori as described by young Henry James. She suddenly felt fearful, that after almost four years, he might reject her and send her away in a rage. Such a thing, she knew, would destroy her beyond repair.

The cotter led her across a tract of cleared land towards the inhabited hovel clinging to the cliff side that she had noticed before. "H-we leave his meals for him once a day. He has a cold breakfast an' a warm supper. He pays us well, too well, for sure." It was suppertime, and he carried a prepared meal in a metal dish that only needed heating awhile on a fire.

They approached the stinking little hovel by a precarious path that cut across a cliff that fell steeply on to the ocean rocks. The smell of salt and seaweed pinched Olive's nostril's as she edged her way along the narrow ledge of the cliff side path

"How did he get up here in the first place?" Olive asked over the crash of the waves below.

"H-an Oirish man in Switzerland told him about it. But Oi tink it's God's work." They were almost at the hovel. "Here, me darlin', ye take this dish to him. Oi'll wait close by in case he gives ye trouble, for h-there's times he don't know what he's doin'."

Olive took the dish, went to the hovel door, knocked, and with a backward glance at the old man, pushed the door open and went inside.

*

Grigori Shum descended from a dark loft above, a ladder dropping into the common room of the cabin - as if it were the inside of a ship. His would be his final descent; he could no longer bear the pain in his head, the penitentiary of his blindness, the knowledge of helplessness. He had often sat listening to the crash of the waves below; he had been warned by old Duggan about the danger of wandering too close to the cliff edge; but he no longer cared, his life was a misery - it was time to end it. He had tried once before, but he had mistaken where the cliff edge had been; instead of throwing himself off as he thought he was doing, he had fallen off a grassy knoll and landed unharmed in a bog. Donal Duggan had found him and helped him back to the cabin, assuming that he had lost his way.

Now, though, Grigori knew exactly where the cliff was it's steepest. Donal had shown him one evening when he had asked to be taken for some fresh air. He had stood above the cliff and felt the rush of sea air blow through his mind. It had been the only moment of happiness he had had since arriving in Ireland. He knew he had come there to die; he did not know when or how, but he knew that when the time came, he would feel it, and know what to do.

The time had come. He kicked over one of the two little red-stained chairs that accompanied a low lame table, which with one flap hanging from a single hinge, looked like a broken wing. A big black pot, some tubs, baskets, and cracked crockery were the only other contents of the cabin room. In a temper, Grigori kicked over the table with the crockery on it and it crashed to the damp earthen floor. He picked up the other red chair and spun it round his head, but the backrest caught on the ceiling crossbeam and broke it. The chair crumbled in his hands. He grabbed hold of the ladder to the loft with the hook on the end of his false arm and wrenched it away. It stuck in the hatch. In a fury, he wrestled with the ladder, swearing and cursing at it, then suddenly, hearing a knock on the cabin door, he went deathly silent.

Olive entered the cabin. There were no windows and no lit candles. She could see nothing, hear nothing. There was a foul odor of fish and excrement. She could sense someone was in the room, for she could hear deep breathing.

Grigori could tell that his visitor was not Donal Duggan. He could smell perfume, sweet scented musk. He suddenly imagined himself stalking a deer, trailing the animal through the forests of the Muscovy, closing in on it, taking the flesh in his hands.

Olive felt a wooden object close round her neck. She stiffened, as a hand wound round her waist. She dropped the dish and tried to bring some words to her lips but none would present themselves. Her arms were forced round her back, and in an instant she found them fastened awkwardly by a chord. She tried to utter Grigori's name, but a filthy cloth was forced into her mouth as a gag and tied behind her head.

Olive began to struggle as a hand began wandering over her dress, into her bodice, under her skirts. She found herself forced face-first to the floor. This could not be Grigori? She began kicking as her petticoats were forced up around her waist, but her knees dug into the mire of the floor as she felt a hand thrust between her buttocks.

"Now, my beauty" she heard in Russian "Donal's sent me a new girl this week." Grigori fell down and placed his knees between her legs, forcing them apart. "What a fine pig you are. I can feel your soft pink flesh. Come on, you little sow, can't you grunt for mad old Grigori." He forced his way into her. "What a fine countess you'd make if you weren't a peasant."

Olive wanted to cry, but how could she? Grigori had become a mere beast of a man, living life at its lowest instinct. It was true; he was mad, utterly insane, and incapable of cleanliness and decent human behaviour. He was on her like a wild animal, scratching her buttocks with his false hand, satisfying his lust in a violent and despicable manner. She gave up struggling.

Grigori grunted and groaned. The pain in his head was like an explosion. He flayed his torso against the flesh of the girl that had been sent to him, but it did not help.

When he had first arrived, the weekly visits by local peasant girls arranged by Donal had helped him to forget the pain, allowed him to find physical release. Not now, not for months. The girl beneath him had momentarily excited him; the binding, that had taken his mind from the pain; the forcing of her legs open, that too had occupied his mind; but the physical consummation, and now the final release, did nothing. The pain was as great as ever.

He extracted himself from the girl on the floor. Suddenly, he could hear the sea again, the crash of the waves. The moment had come. He threw open the cabin door and took a deep breath of sea-air. The tide was in.

Donal Duggan, lying in the grass waiting for something to happen, saw Grigori lunge out of the cabin and into the early grey of the night. He stood up immediately. He knew something was wrong, for Grigori was running along the cliff path, occasionally stumbling, heading towards the big cliff. There was no sign of his 'wife'.

Donal was in two minds. "Chesus, he's goin' to kill himsel'. He's goin' to kill me golden goose." He began running after Grigori, for Donal Duggan had come to rely heavily on the money his tenant paid to him for 'services'. He had tried to find out where the blind man hid his money, so too had the girls he had sent him, but they'd had not a bit of luck. Then Donal thought "H- what about her? Chesus, I hope he hasn't killed the girl. Oi'll get the blame for leavin' her with that mad eggit." He stopped and stood motionless and in a dither as to which one of them to go to first. "Chesus, Donal Duggan, ye whore-master!" he chastised himself "H-what have Oi done to that poor sweet girl"

Donal returned to the cabin and entered to find Olive sitting upright on the unbroken red chair. She had managed to undo her bonds and re-arrange her clothing. "Chesus, yer alright, lass" He was relieved nothing untoward had happened to her. "Quick, get up now, help me get him off the big cliff."

Olive was shaken. The violent act against her had not sent her into hysterics. She had come to expect such things from men - it had happened for the first time with her Turkish master, and then repeatedly, by his sons and their friends. It was something she had told no one except Mrs. Milosovic in Belgrade who had seen the scars on her back and buttocks were she had been repeatedly flogged by her master. That part of her body was not beautiful; no one ever saw it except Clarissa who had been told that it was a childhood accident.

Olive followed Donal Duggan along the cliff path. Grigori had not yet reached the big cliff. They could not see him stumble and fall. He was out of view. Somehow, he was managing without sight to find his way out along the ridge.

Duggan and Olive thought they were gaining on him. He came into view. "Chesus, he's reached the big cliff. Look!"

Olive saw Grigori standing on the edge of the cliff. It was Grigori all right, she could not mistake his massive build. In the cabin she had not seen him at all, only felt the power of his hands, and the will of his body. Now, seeing him perched on the edge of a hundred foot cliff, the Atlantic waves licking at its base, she felt a great sense of awe. Here, at last, was Grigori Shum, Count Rostov, the man who had made her what she was - here, was that same man, come down in the world, reduced to the peasant existence from which she had escaped. He was blind, broken and without hope, yet, there was something majestic in his bearing, something quintessentially noble and heroic in his choice of end.

"Chesus, he's goin' to jump" shouted Duggan "We can still stop him!"

Olive held the old man by the arm. "No!" she cried.

Donal Duggan did not protest, he knew that the end had come for the mad-man, that he could not continue to live as he had done. The money had been very useful, but he knew that it could not go on forever. He resigned himself to watch his golden goose kill itself.

Grigori raised his arms to the heavens. Twilight was coming on and he made a shadow against the darkening western sky. There was no red sunset, only a faint band of white light that was quickly narrowing, and it was by the light cast by this narrowing ribbon of light, that Olive watched as Grigori tossed himself over the cliff. She turned away as his body hit the rocks, then looked back to catch the waves washing his body into the sea.

Old Duggan took Olive by the arm. "Come, me lass, Oi'll take ye back to me cot. Ye can stay with me 'til he floats ashore. The sea always washes up it's dead, and soon enough we'll find him on the shingle."
Duggan led Olive off the cliff and back to the cottage where Clarissa and Michael Cormack the cabbie were waiting. She neither cried nor appeared to be in shock. She was calm for the first time since learning in America that Grigori was still alive.

*

They found Grigori the following morning on the bay sands barely a hundred yards from Duggan's cottage. His false arm was missing. They wrapped him in some old bed sheets and took him back to Sligo in the carriage, then on to Galway in a coffin. Two days later there was a small service in the church of St. Nicholas, and Grigori was buried in the churchyard alongside sailors and thieves.
That night, an unearthly afterglow lingered in the sky, a dull red haze hung over the hills like dust flung from carriage wheels. The edges of the Atlantic were washed in a pale green colour that melted into the blue of the dusk. As the light drew out of the sky, a few stars rose over the steel-blue heights of Connemara. It was a strange beauty, a velvet softness that did not seem to belong to any part of the world that Olive had ever seen. It belonged wholly to itself, to Galway, to a part of Olive's life which was over.

21

It had been Olive's intention to return to America, but her own illness had taken a turn for the worse when she had a stroke while staying with the Irish James's in County Cavan. At first it was all the old symptoms she had in Newport, which, in part, were alleviated by a strict sugar-free diet and a return to eating raw garlic. This prompted many jokes amongst the James's, in particular from Aunt Barbara (the cousin that Henry Senior had fallen in love with when he had visited twenty years earlier), but this soon stopped when it was discovered that Olive was pregnant.

At first it came as a shock to Olive herself, for she had totally blocked out from her mind the experience she had undergone in the Drumcliff hovel. She had forgiven Grigori's madness and negated his attack on her by convincing herself that she was his wife, and that no crime had been committed. The doctor, an Edinburgh man, told her that she would die if she had a baby because her illness had increased her blood pressure and induced the likelihood of further strokes. Her kidneys were already badly damaged, and that, said the doctor, was reason enough to terminate the pregnancy.

Olive refused. She was a catholic. She could not take the life of her own baby. Besides, she would be having Grigori's baby. Her life meant nothing. She had achieved more than had ever been expected from a peasant girl. She had experienced so much so early in life that it seemed natural that her life should be brought to an early end.

Such talk frightened the James's, a protestant family who held steadfastly in the belief that man determined his own future and that life had little to do with the forces of fate. Olive, however, believed that God had intervened and given her seven wonderful years in lieu of having Grigori's child. She never for a moment considered that it might have been the work of the devil that had placed her on high; the notion that she had sold her soul, as Dr. Faust had done, it was a concept beyond her imagination; deep down she thought of herself as a simple peasant girl who had done none any harm.

Perhaps it is strange that those who believe in God most sometimes turn out to be the least angel like. Before her illness, Olive had never been a great believer in the power of God. Now, as she lay, day after day, in bed, reading what she could, writing letters to Henry James, Sisi, William Howells, and to Abraham Lincoln, she felt more and more the presence of a force she had until then been unaware of. She began to hear, then see, the many spirits of the past, for the James's lived in a grand old Irish house some centuries old, visited by Oliver Cromwell during his Irish campaign. Olive spoke with Cromwell; at first he was just a shadowy figure amongst the other visitors that came to Olive in the night, and she did not know whom he was. Then, by chance, one of the James's gave her a book on the history of the Irish peoples, and there, inside, was a portrait of the man she had been seeing at the foot of her bed. She did not like him; he was an evil spirit who tried to get her to rid herself of her baby. He told her to throw herself down the stairs, or to pick up a candleholder and to beat herself in the stomach, but she would not listen to him, she would drive him away with stern words and admonishments.

Clarissa was never far away. The shouts of her mistress in the night disturbed her to the extent that she moved her own bed into Olive's room and slept by her, but things became so bad, that the whole household came to be disturbed. Eventually, the doctor arranged for Olive to be moved. It was his opinion that all physical remedies had been applied, and that more stringent spiritual ones were required if the patient was to keep her sanity. So after a month at the James's house, she was taken by invalid carriage to a convent hospital in Meath.

*

The first morning Olive woke in the convent of the Sisters of Our Lady she heard a noisy bell ringing down the corridor. Her door opened and Sister Gabriella looked in on her smiling, wishing her good morning, a bowl of bathing water in one hand and a bell in the other. It was six a.m.

Olive was expected to rise and was chided for neglecting to pull herself out of bed.

"But I am not well" replied Olive feebly.

The Sister shook her head as if Olive had

said something wrong. It was her Sister creed to help every stranger no matter how low they had fallen, as though they were the Blessed Mary herself, but they also had to help themselves.

Sister Gabriella drew the curtains and the sun leapt into Olive's cell. The garden was beautiful with silver dew on the grass and awkward early morning shadows over everything.

As Olive looked out she saw a wonderful sight. A small deer came gingerly across the grass leaving a black track in the dew. She halted below Olive's window, lifted her ears and listened. Olive thought of St. Francis. She wondered if the sisters had tamed this most timid creature. The deer dropped her ears and louped out of sight.

As Olive washed she smelt the burning of a pipe. Thin wisps of grey tobacco smoke blew into her cell. It was Turkish tobacco; Constantinople immediately filled her thoughts, the sweet aromatic smell that had been everywhere. Someone was smoking on the porch beneath her window. She looked down and saw directly below her a head of straggly gray hair, that of an agued middle-aged woman struggling to lift a pipe to her mouth. She too was a guest in the convent. This, then, thought Olive was the pitiful creature Margaret whose tortured voice had woken her in the middle of the night screaming "O Mary, mother of God, I want a drink ...." which she had repeated six or seven times, appealing to different saints, not for milk or water, but for alcohol.

While Margaret stood there smoking furtively, a sister came through the convent garden and onwards down the straight path. It was Sister Gabriella, the guest-sister and curer of drunkards. As soon as she was spotted, the pipe was hastily knocked against the wall and tossed into a bush. Margaret straightened, shuffled and took on a stance of innocence. Sister Gabriella came up in long strides, the toes of her thick shoes wet with dew.

"Good morning" she cried cheerfully "and how are you this morning, Margaret?"

"Oh, sister", she replied in a cringing voice "I'm bad, I'm that bad ... I had the devils at me all night."

"And why then didn't ye wake me, Margaret?" asked the sister solemnly. "Sure, I'd have come to ye in an instant and calmed ye."

"I was wan to wake ye, sister. Ye've been so fine to me."

Margaret raised her trembling hand to her brow. Sister Gabriella placed a friendly hand on her shoulder and spoke to her as a mother would a child. "Well, never ye mind now ... Come, I'll give ye a little drop just to take the edge off yer thirst."

They went into together and Olive heard the turn of a key in a cabinet door. Later, Olive would discover, that Sister Gabriella was one of the greatest living experts in the treatment of dipsomania. She gave drunkards the amount of liquor to which they were accustomed, but she reduced the quantities every day until at the end of the cure, they were drinking water.

As for Olive's cure, there was none yet invented. She had a disorder that had long been diagnosed but which none had found a cure for. In twenty, thirty, or even fifty years time perhaps some smart physician would stumble upon a solution that would save lives. It was known that it ran in families and that a virus or other trauma brought it on. It was also known that sugar in the blood built up and damaged blood vessels and other organs. It was called *diabetes mellitus* and Olive's own mother had died from the same disorder when she was an infant.

Olive's thirst was much different from that of Margaret in the cell below her. Because of her disorder, she had to constantly urinate which left her dehydrated. She was thus encouraged by Sister Gabriela to drink enormous quantities of water every day to flush her system of the excess sugars in her blood. Contrary to the doctor's advice, it was the sister's experience that constant daily exercise also helped the condition by keeping her circulation going.

"Yer pins and needles in yer fingers and toes are a result of bad circulation, that's why ye have bad sores." The sister was very direct "So, I'll have none of yer excuses. Ye'll get out of bed at six a.m., or I'll be sending for the doctor in a month's time to cut yer feet off because of gangrene."

The thought of losing her feet made Olive take the sister's advice seriously. In spite of her fatigue, she rose every morning with the bell, and later in the morning was accompanied by Sister Gabriella in a long circuitous walk during which they talked about everything under the sun. She knew she was not improving; everyday the walk became more difficult, but she was grateful that with the sister's care she would live long enough to give birth. Thankfully, the spirits that had been visiting her at the James's house, no longer did so at the convent, she slept peacefully, remembering little of her dreams.

The months passed. Clarissa had been instructed to take up service with the James's, but she had not done so, she had remained at the convent to help the sisters anyway she could. She assisted her mistress whenever she was needed, taking the place of Sister Gabriella when she was not free to go for walks. She enjoyed the routine of the convent, made many friends amongst the sisters, and for the first time in her life, felt happy. Naturally, she was sad about the condition of her mistress, and cried many times before her, and on her own with Sister Gabriella, fearing what was to become of her once her mistress was gone. Olive told her to have faith in Sister Gabriella, and Sister Gabriella told her to have faiths in God, and between them, they managed to prepare Clarissa for Olive's end.

Towards the end of summer, Olive lost her sight, the small blood vessels in her eyes destroyed by her disorder. She bore her new handicap with the knowledge that Grigori had also been without his sight, and through it, she tried to understand how he might have felt. It was a strange sensation to wake and find that one blackness replaced another. She could make out fleeting shadows when people stood before her in the sunlight; occasionally there would be bright flashes of red or blue light on her lids; but most of the time, there was a grey-black gloom which she could only disperse by remembering the glorious colours of the Laxenburg blossoms, or the White House roses.

She had to dictate her letters to Clarissa or Sister Gabriella. During her stay at the convent she had built up steady correspondence with her friends overseas. When the letters from the Empress of Austria arrived, there was always a flurry of excitement in the convent, not least Clarissa, who was always eager to hear something of home. As they were written in German, Clarissa was the only one able to read them aloud:

Dearest Olive Vanya,
I am back now from Corfu, an enchanting and delightful place that I am determined to make my winter home. Franz Josef is still a little cold but he is trying to be warmer and I think he really does love me. I am now allowed to see the children as ma-in-law is very ill and likely to die. I feel for Franz Josef for he adores his mother, but I will not be sorry to see her go. As you know she has done a lot to damage our marriage and I cannot forgive her even as she lies on her deathbed.
I am so glad you are with child, but

*saddened to hear that you are not better
for it. Why ever are you in a convent in
Ireland? Can't you come home to Vienna?
Marie misses you as much as I do ......*

Clarissa read on but Olive burst into tears.
She had thought that she had not missed
Vienna, but deep down she had; she
missed her friends Sisi and Marie; she
missed the gaiety of the court; but more
than all, she regretted her abandonment of
singing. She could not remember the last
time that she had sung
"Madeira" said Clarissa firmly.
"Surely not that long?"
"Yes, mam ... the night you embarrassed
Mister Howells."
It all seemed long ago. In between, there
had been Vienna, Venice, Boston,
Washington, and then Ireland, poor, sick
old Ireland, where she lay blind and near
death. It was only the kick of the baby in
her belly that kept her going, stopped her
from 'giving up the ghost' as Sister
Gabriella put it.
Then, at six a.m. on a clear August morning
as Sister Gabriella rang her bell, Olive gave
birth. The ordeal went on all day and long
into the night, and there was the fear that
the baby might be lost. The physician was
sent for, and by caesarian, he delivered a
girl. Everyone in the room was overjoyed.
The baby was placed in Olive's arms, and
the first thing she did was run her fingers
over the child's face.
"Is he just like Grigori?"
"It's a girl, my dear", replied Sister

Gabriella.

"Is she like me then?"

"She looks just like the master, mam" interceded Clarissa.

Olive began humming a tune to the baby, then added words. It was the same song she had sung for Grigori in Vienna on the first, then his last night with her, a Viennese tune with Russian words. Sister Gabriella, Clarissa, the doctor, and some of the other nuns who had come to know Olive, fell silent, mesmerized by the lullaby qualities of the *Blue Danube* tune and Olive's singing.

Suddenly, the song ended. Clarissa threw her arms around her mistresses, demanding she speak to her. There was no reply from Olive. Her face had fixed into a beautiful smile, the baby lying in her arms.

*

They mourned Olive's passing with great reverence and had her buried in the specially prepared vault in the convent. The vault had been planned some months in advance of her death and Olive had been allowed to chose its location beneath a cypress tree. She had left the convent the bulk of the forty-five thousand dollars (much of which she had invested in Trans-Pacific railroad stock - an investment tip she had been given by Henry James). She put in trust for her child the thirty thousand pounds Grigori had left. Grigori had been wise enough to leave most of his money in Dublin before renting the cabin in County Sligo, for he had never trusted anyone, and trusted even less his own abilities to hold on to his money after he was blind. He had made a will and named the Countess Rostov as sole beneficiary, so that even to his end, Grigori Shum had kept up the pretence that Olive was his wife.

Arrangements had been made to bring the child up in the convent. Sister Gabriella was to be the child's guardian, until she reached the age of twenty-one. They baptised her Elizabeth Shum; Sister Gabriella always called her Elizabeth, while Clarissa always addressed her as Sissy.

As for Clarissa herself, after a short stay in Cashel, she returned to the convent to become a novice, and then took her vows. Every day, spring through autumn, she laid fresh flowers at the vault of Olive Vanya. In the winter months when blooms were scarce, she arranged small bouquets of berried evergreens in the manner of a wreath and laid those in place of flowers. Only once in twenty-one years did she fail to make her daily visit the vault, and that was the day she had fallen and broken her arm on ice when carrying Sissy.

Clarissa's devotion to her mistress was recognised by all who knew her. The end for the young countess had been so tragic, and the service of her servant after death, was no less so. Yet, there was some secret that Clarissa kept from them all.

Some time after Olive's burial, the remains of Grigori were disinterred from the churchyard of St. Nicholas in Galway where he was buried with thieves and sailors, and re-interred with Olive Vanya in the beautiful convent grounds in Meath.

And so it came to pass that Olive Vanya came to lie with her beloved Count beneath the big skies and the green grass of Ireland, some seven years after she had first met and fallen in love with him. He had perished through madness and suicide, she by illness and childbirth, yet through it all, they had produced a daughter who by rights would inherit the earth.

Through their daughter, Olive and Grigori would continue their love.

ROBBIE MOFFAT

The author was born and schooled in Glasgow. He took a degree in English language and Literature at Newcastle University. He began writing when he was seventeen and has a had a career as a poet, novelist, playwright and screenwriter. He is best known for his feature film work in which he is also a director and producer.

His prose writing as been overshadowed by this. He wrote his first novel when he was twenty two and continued to write novels for the next twenty years. None of them were published.

The rediscovery of his prose work has lead to a recent spate of publications that has lead to a resurgence of interest in his prose work.